# xoxo, Betty and Veronica

## In Each Other's Shoes

by Adrianne Ambrose

Grosset & Dunlap
An Imprint of Penguin Group (USA) Inc.

GROSSET & DUNLAP
Published by the Penguin Group
Penguin Group (USA) Inc., 375 Hudson Street,
New York, New York 10014, USA
Penguin Group (Canada), 90 Eglinton Avenue East, Suite 700,
Toronto, Ontario M4P 2Y3, Canada (a division of Pearson Penguin Canada Inc.)
Penguin Books Ltd., 80 Strand, London WC2R 0RL, England
Penguin Group Ireland, 25 St. Stephen's Green, Dublin 2,
Ireland (a division of Penguin Books Ltd.)
Penguin Group (Australia), 250 Camberwell Road, Camberwell,
Victoria 3124, Australia (a division of Pearson Australia Group Pty. Ltd.)
Penguin Books India Pvt. Ltd., 11 Community Centre,
Panchsheel Park, New Delhi—110 017, India
Penguin Group (NZ), 67 Apollo Drive, Rosedale, Auckland 0632,
New Zealand (a division of Pearson New Zealand Ltd.)
Penguin Books (South Africa) (Pty.) Ltd., 24 Sturdee Avenue,
Rosebank, Johannesburg 2196, South Africa

Penguin Books Ltd., Registered Offices: 80 Strand,
London WC2R 0RL, England

Published by Grosset & Dunlap, a division of Penguin Young Readers Group,
345 Hudson Street, New York, New York 10014. GROSSET & DUNLAP is a
trademark of Penguin Group (USA) Inc. Printed in the U.S.A.

ISBN 978-0-448-45712-3          10 9 8 7 6 5 4 3 2 1

"Hey, Betty!" Veronica called. "Wait up." She hustled down the hall to catch up with her best friend, her mile-high heels click, click, clicking on the linoleum floor of Riverdale High School.

Betty shook her head with bewildered amusement, causing her long, blond ponytail to swing. "I don't know how you do it, Ronnie."

"Do what?"

"Wear those stilettos all day." Betty nodded toward her friend's designer shoes. "Aren't your feet killing you?"

"Dah-ling," Veronica said, doing her best to sound like a Hungarian socialite, "zees are Giammos. Zhey are wary, wary chic."

"Huh?" Betty wasn't sure what her friend was talking about.

"They're Giammos," Veronica explained, slipping back into her own, middle-American accent. "Your feet could hurt so bad you think they're going to fall off, but you have to keep wearing them."

Betty looked down at the shoes. They were pretty cute, but not worth losing a foot or anything. No shoes were that cute. "Why?"

"Fashion," Veronica said as if her one-word answer made everything clear.

Betty shrugged. Mr. Lodge, Veronica's wealthy father, indulged his only daughter with numerous credit cards for which he promised to always pay the balance. Veronica took him at his word and bought designer clothes by the pound. She did look great all the time. Still, Betty thought, teetering around the school on stilts all day was just too painful and way too silly. Betty looked down at her own feet. She had on a pair of brown ankle boots that were supercute and supercomfy that she had found on sale for 50 percent off.

After opening her locker, Betty piled her math and history books on the shelf, and then yanked out her book for social studies. Veronica stood nearby, peering into a compact and freshening her lipstick. "What are you doing after school?" she asked, making a small kissy face in the mirror to even out the color.

"There's a meeting for *The Blue and Gold*," Betty told her.

Veronica did her best not to roll her eyes. Writing for Riverdale High's newspaper sounded megaboring to her, but if Betty liked it, she wasn't going to judge. "Well, I just heard that Ms. Crouton is choosing someone to organize the school's charity fashion show this afternoon. It's coming up, you know."

"Oh," Betty replied.

"Wouldn't you rather go to the fashion meeting? I just know Ms. Crouton is going to pick me to head up the committee, and I'm going to need a ton of help. It's going to be so much fun! Don't you want to go?"

"Uh, no. Not really," Betty said, trying to make her rejection as gentle as possible.

3

"But tell you what. When we get closer to the fashion show, I'll write an article in *The Blue and Gold* to promote it."

Fluffing up her black bangs, Veronica chuckled to herself. She never read the school newspaper and was pretty sure no one else did, either. But Betty enjoyed it, and there was no persuading her otherwise. "Okay, that sounds . . . um . . . great," she said, snapping shut the compact and then slipping it back into her bag.

XOXO

Betty loved being a writer for *The Blue and Gold*. It was just so much fun crafting articles like a real journalist. Even if sometimes the articles were about proper lunchroom etiquette or that time the gym teacher twisted his knee trying to show his students how to climb a rope. Ms. Grundy, the faculty advisor for the school paper, had mentioned that there would be a big announcement at the afternoon meeting. Betty couldn't even begin to imagine what would constitute a "big" announcement.

After her last class of the day, Betty rushed to the school's newspaper office. Sometimes the newspaper's meetings could be sparsely attended. Especially if there was something else going on like a pep rally or a dance committee meeting. But not this time. The room was packed. Everyone was curious about Ms. Grundy's "big announcement."

"What do you think is going on?" Betty asked, slipping into a seat next to Ginger Lopez.

"No idea," Ginger said as she vigorously brushed her two-toned hair. She had a luxurious expanse of rich, chestnut-brown hair, but she always kept her bangs tinted blond. Her look wasn't exactly the style at Riverdale High, but Ginger worked part-time as a teen editor for *Sparkle Magazine* in New York City, so no one dared question her fashion choices. "There are only two issues left to put out this year. I hope they're not going to announce anything crazy like we're not doing them due to budget cuts or something."

"Oh, they wouldn't do that, do you think?"

Ms. Grundy stood up and walked to the front of the room so everyone immediately stopped chatting and settled down. "I'm glad so many of you decided to attend the meeting today because we have a very important decision to make," she said. "I'm sorry to say that *The Blue and Gold*'s current editor in chief, Larry Parks, will be leaving us very soon because his mother has been transferred to Indianapolis. Therefore, we have to decide on a new editor for the last two issues of the school newspaper."

The room immediately began to buzz as students discussed the sudden departure of Larry and the vacancy it would create. Betty felt her heartbeat quicken. Being a reporter for *The Blue and Gold* was one thing, but to actually be the editor in chief? That would be a dream come true.

"A-hem." Ms. Grundy gave a stern clearing of her throat. "Settle, everyone, settle," she said as if the students were an unruly pack of Irish setters. "First of all, do we have any nominations for a new editor?"

Betty scanned the room, trying desperately to make eye contact with anyone who might possibly nominate her. Her eyes locked on Kevin Keller, who was nonchalantly leaning against a bookshelf. She turned up the full wattage on her baby blues, pleading with him to please, please, please say her name. Seamlessly taking the hint, Kevin raised his hand and said in a casual tone, "I nominate Betty Cooper."

Betty felt her face go bright red. Ms. Grundy looked over at her. "Do you accept the nomination, Betty?"

"Yes," Betty said, her voice cracking slightly. She hoped she didn't sound too eager, but she couldn't stop beaming. "Definitely."

A second later, Ginger Lopez shot her hand into the air. "I nominate myself."

"Can you do that?" Chuck Clayton wondered from the far corner of the room. He was the paper's cartoonist, but he still felt invested in getting a good editor.

"Of course you can," Ginger replied. "Or at least I can. I mean, after all, I'm the only one here with actual professional journalism experience."

As soon as Ms. Grundy agreed that Ginger's nomination was permissible, there was a rash of student self-nominations. It took just thirty seconds for there to be six candidates vying for the position of *The Blue and Gold*'s editor in chief.

"Oh, dear," said Ms. Grundy. She had hoped for one or maybe even two reasonably qualified students to want the position. She hadn't expected to have to decide between half a dozen. "I guess we'll have to put it to a vote."

"That sounds good to me," Ginger said, getting to her feet. "Everyone who wants me for editor, raise your hand."

"Not that kind of vote," Ms. Grundy said sharply, interrupting the impromptu proceedings. "I meant an official school vote. There are school elections tomorrow, and we'll just make this part of the ballots."

# Chapter 2

Veronica drummed her fingers on the desk in front of her. Ms. Crouton, the home economics teacher and faculty advisor to the fashion show, was late. "What can she be doing?" she said half to herself and half to Midge Klump, who was sitting at the desk next to hers.

"Maybe some kind of soufflé emergency," Midge joked, shrugging her petite shoulders.

Scanning the room, Veronica took in the other girls that had shown up for the first fashion show meeting. Her competition. Or the lack thereof. Veronica assured herself that she was the obvious choice to organize the show. Ms. Crouton only had to look at

9

their handbags alone to know that Veronica had more fashion to decorate her little finger with than some of the girls had in their whole wardrobes.

Ms. Crouton bustled in. "Sorry I'm late." She dumped a large armful of papers, recipe books, and fabric swatches on her desk. "So," she said in a getting-down-to-business voice, "it's only six weeks until Riverdale High School's charity fashion show to raise money for the children's hospital. I don't know about any of you, but it's my favorite event of the year." Several of the girls nodded in agreement. "There is a lot of work to get done," Ms. Crouton continued. "We have to find vendors, and we have to pick a theme. But first of all, I need to pick a student to head the fashion show. Are there any volunteers?"

Of the dozen and a half girls that showed up for the meeting, seven hands immediately shot into the air. Veronica let out a little gasp. She couldn't help it. Wasn't it painfully obvious to everyone in the room that she was the only real choice to be in charge of the fashion show? Unable to restrain herself, Veronica blurted, "Ms. Crouton?"

"Yes?" The teacher looked over at her.

"I think it's pretty obvious that there's only one girl at Riverdale that's really qualified to head up the charity fashion show."

"Why, thank you, Veronica," Ginger said, breezing into the room. "I accept your nomination. That's so sweet of you."

"What?" Veronica was stunned. "What are you talking about? I didn't mean you."

"Really?" Ginger feigned surprise. "I heard you say that there was only one obvious choice in the whole school to head the show, so I naturally assumed you meant me."

Veronica folded her arms. "Why would you assume that?"

"Well, there are plenty of girls in this school who are fashionable," Ginger said with a superior smirk. "But as far as I know, I'm the only one who actually works in fashion."

"So?" Veronica kept her arms folded.

"Don't you get it?" Ginger laughed as if it was so obvious. "I write the articles that dictate what fashionistas such as yourself actually wear. I'm the one that creates fashion. That's why I'm the obvious choice for the job. I mean, really, who do you think should head up the show? A girl who follows fashion or a girl who creates it?"

Ginger's comments must have rubbed most of the girls at the meeting the wrong way because there was an outburst of angry chatter when no one could get a word in edgewise. Ms. Crouton held both her hands up in the air. "Girls, please! Quiet!" The chatter faded to a dull roar. "It's admirable that so many of you are eager to participate in charity work. So I think the only way to choose a committee head fairly is to do it by school-wide vote."

"What?!" both Veronica and Ginger said simultaneously.

XOXO

"Can you believe Ginger?" Veronica asked, refilling Betty's glass with lemonade. The Lodge family naturally had a butler on hand to do such things, but Veronica felt that sometimes it was nice to have a conversation without the staff standing there listening. "I mean, as if I would nominate her."

"Well, you're not going to believe this," Betty said, adding a bit of sugar to her drink, "but Ginger's also running for editor in chief of *The Blue and Gold*."

"I thought Larry was the editor."

"He's moving to Indianapolis," Betty explained.

Veronica thought about it. "Oh, that's too bad. Larry's cute, and I've never had the chance to go on a date with him."

"Geez, Ronnie." Betty laughed. "You've already got half the boys in the school lining up to take you out. You don't have to go on a date with every single one."

"I can try."

The girls laughed, but Betty knew Veronica preferred Archie Andrews over any other boy in the school. Even though they weren't dating exclusively or anything. She was free to go out with whomever she wanted. It's true that half her dates were strategically staged to make Archie jealous, but he didn't know that.

"You should have heard Ginger at the meeting," Betty continued. "She practically threw it in everyone's face that she works at *Sparkle Magazine*. I mean, if it's so great working there, why does she want to work on the school paper?"

"She was bragging about *Sparkle* at the fashion show meeting, too!" Veronica exclaimed. "I mean, I love *Sparkle* and everything, but it's not the final word in fashion."

Betty took a big gulp of lemonade and set down her glass. "You know what? I hope you get the fashion show and I get the paper. We both deserve it."

Veronica nodded her head enthusiastically. "Wouldn't that be awesome? And it would definitely show Ginger."

# Chapter 3

"Vote for Ginger," Ginger Lopez said, handing Nancy Woods a bright red campaign button.

Nancy was wearing a fetching yellow dress that made her mocha skin all but glow. Nancy considered the fashion option of adding the red button to her ensemble. "Vote for Ginger for what?" she asked.

"Everything."

"No, seriously," Nancy pressed. "I have no idea what you're running for."

"I'm running for everything," Ginger explained without a hint of sarcasm.

"Everything?" Chuck Clayton asked, slipping his arm around Nancy's trim waist.

"Well," Ginger conceded, "everything that matters." Then, a little impatiently, she added, "Oh, come on, Chuck. You were at the meeting. You know I'm running for editor of *The Blue and Gold*."

Nancy looked at her boyfriend. "Why aren't you running for editor? Or me, for that matter?"

Shrugging, Chuck told her, "I'm too happy being the cartoonist for the paper. Being editor would just get in the way."

With a laugh, Nancy nuzzled him. "That's my honey."

"And you're not running"—he thought about it—"because you skipped the last meeting, I guess. I wanted to nominate you, but I wasn't sure if you'd have time to be editor with all your other activities."

"Oh, that's sweet." Nancy nuzzled him.

"I'm also running to head the charity fashion show," Ginger hurriedly added. She didn't need Chuck and Nancy getting all cuddly wuddly in front of where she had set up to greet potential voters. "Have a button,

Chuck." She thrust a VOTE FOR GINGER button at him. "See you guys later!" she added briskly, nudging them down the hall.

Betty trotted up the front steps of Riverdale High, riffling through her papers, looking for her math homework. "Betty!" Someone called out her name.

"Hey, Ronnie. What's up?" she asked as her best friend pulled her to one side.

"Look," Veronica whispered, nodding toward the school's main hallway. "Ginger's campaigning."

Betty squinted in the direction indicated. "Wow. She must have stayed up all night making those posters."

"And she's handing out buttons." This caused her best friend to giggle. "What's so funny?" Veronica asked.

"I was just wondering how she got buttons so quickly. I mean, does she have a boxful in the back of her closet in case she decides to suddenly run for something or what?"

Veronica folded her arms and glared down the hall. "I wouldn't put it past her."

## XOXO

Jughead Jones wasn't a fan of hard work. He was more of a fan of snacking, relaxing, napping, and just plain taking it easy. A life of extreme leisure was fine by him. But in a school like Riverdale, where everyone was always participating in everything, Jughead found it hard to maintain his status as a low-profile loaf. People were always trying to get him to join teams and sign up for clubs. Jughead found it very stressful. Still, as a student, he had an obligation to participate a little bit. And it was always a good idea to have at least some activities to list on college applications.

So Jughead kept his eyes open for low-impact activities that wouldn't heavily impede any kind of snacking opportunities that might arise. Monitoring the ballot boxes during a school election was right up his alley. The gist of the job was just sitting at a table that was covered with boxes. Ostensibly, he was there to keep people from cheating or answer any questions they might have. But it was only a minor election, so the chance that anyone would be desperate enough to cheat was minimal. And there were the names of each category taped on the lid of each box, so the voting procedure was pretty self-explanatory. The only thing that bothered Jughead about the whole process was why anyone would go out of their way to run for a school office in the first place.

"How's it going, Jugglehead?" Reggie asked, sidling up to the ballot boxes. A small line had formed as Riverdale's students dropped by at the end of the school day to cast their votes.

"Not bad," Jughead replied. "Just taking her easy."

"How are the elections going? Anyone tried to stuff the ballot box yet or anything?" Reggie asked, sliding a ballot in the box labeled NEW FOOTBALL UNIFORMS. Seeing that Reggie was on the team and always keen to impress the girls, it was no mystery as to how he would vote.

"Not yet," Jughead replied. He had his feet propped up on the desk and his ever-present crown-shaped beanie pushed forward to keep the glare from the overhead lights out of his eyes. "Ginger Lopez has been by here, like, a dozen times to ask me how I think the votes are going, but I always have to tell her that as Ballot Master, I can't reveal that information."

Reggie chuckled. "That's what this job is called? Collecting ballots makes you a Ballot Master?"

After giving it some thought, Jughead replied, "I don't know what the official title is, but that's what I've been calling it. I thought Ballot Overlord sounded a little too intimidating."

Reggie worked his way through the eight ballot boxes, systematically casting his votes. "I'm surprised you volunteered for this, Juggler. Especially today."

"Why's that?" Jughead wondered, not particularly interested.

"Because of the library bake sale. I mean, don't you usually like to get in on those things?"

Jughead sat up. "The library is having a

bake sale?" He abruptly dropped his feet to the floor. "Today?"

"Yeah. Didn't you know?" Reggie exited the voting line. Smoothing down his shiny black hair, he used his reflection in a trophy case to check his appearance.

Jughead suddenly felt very, very unsatisfied with his position as Ballot Master. If he had realized there was a bake sale conflict, he would have never, ever volunteered. "Were you by there? Is Ms. Crouton there? Did she bake her chocolate doughnuts?"

"Sure." Reggie licked his lips. "I had two. Wow, are those things good!"

"Good?!" Jughead yelped. "They're the most delicious things on this planet! They're maybe even as good as hamburgers!" He got to his feet and began pacing back and forth behind the voting table. "Were there any left?"

Reggie shrugged. "Sure, there were some left. I mean, not a ton, but there never are."

"How long is the bake sale going to last?"

"I don't know," Reggie told him. "How long do bake sales usually last?"

Grabbing the front of his friend's shirt, Jughead all but pleaded, "Reggie, you've got to do me a favor."

"Easy, Jughead," Reggie said, shaking him off. "Nothing's that important."

"Oh, yes, it is!" Jughead insisted. "You have to watch the ballot booth for me! Just for five minutes so I can go get a doughnut."

Reggie was reluctant. "Oh, I don't know. I've got kind of a date, and I don't want to be late or anything."

"Please!" Jughead whined. "Five minutes. All I'm asking is for five minutes!"

Rolling his eyes, Reggie gave in. "Okay, fine. What do I have to do?"

"Do? Nothing! You don't have to do anything!" Jughead took off running down the hall toward the library. "All you have to do is sit there!" he shouted over his shoulder.

A couple of students were walking away as Jughead ran toward the bake sale table that was set up outside the library. He gave them a quick scan to see if either was enjoying baked goods. "Ms. Crouton!" Jughead gasped as he made it up to the table. "You're helping with the library bake sale!"

The home economics teacher gave him a quizzical look. "Of course, Jughead. Didn't you get the e-mail I sent to remind you?"

"You sent me an e-mail?" Jughead asked, adjusting his beanie and catching his breath.

"Of course I did." The teacher smiled. "You're our best customer for these things."

"Oh. I haven't read my e-mail in a few weeks," Jughead admitted. "I can't remember the password."

"Don't you just hate that?" Ms. Crouton shook her head ruefully. "I usually write some clues to myself on a piece of paper to keep around for the first few weeks in case I forget."

"Yeah, I do that, too," Jughead agreed. "But then I forget where I put the piece of paper."

Ms. Crouton couldn't help but laugh. Gesturing toward the baked goods piled on the table, she said, "So, Jughead, what can I get you today?"

Jughead felt around in his pockets, pulling

out a movie stub, a crumpled dollar bill, and some lint. "Three of your extra special chocolate doughnuts, please."

The teacher looked dubious. "Doughnuts are seventy-five cents apiece," she informed him. "You know that."

"Yeah," Jughead said sheepishly, "but I was kind of hoping I could get a little credit."

"Oh no. Not after last time." Ms. Crouton was adamant. "No credit, no collateral, no barter system. You want a doughnut, you pay for a doughnut."

Jughead's reputation as a mooch had obviously extended even to the faculty of Riverdale High. "That's disappointing," he said, forking over his dollar and grabbing a doughnut dripping with chocolate glaze. "How much longer is the bake sale going on?" His words were slightly muffled because he'd already taken a giant bite out of the pastry.

"We'll go for another twenty minutes. Maybe thirty."

"But I've got to watch the voting booth for another twenty minutes," Jughead wailed. "I'll

24

never be able to deliver the ballots to the office, find someone to lend me some money, and get back here in time. And these doughnuts are the most perfect food on earth!"

Ms. Crouton was flattered. She knew her doughnuts were good, but no one had ever called them the most perfect food on earth. "Tell you what," she said, patting him on the shoulder. "I'll definitely keep the booth open for the full thirty minutes. But after that, I'm leaving. Teachers have lives outside of school, too, you know."

"Thanks, Ms. Crouton!" Jughead called over his shoulder. He was already running back toward the voting booth. Reggie usually had money on him for such dire emergencies.

But as Jughead approached the voting booth, scarfing down the last few bites of his doughnut as he ran, it was very clear that Reggie would not be inclined to lend him a few dollars. "I thought you said just five minutes!" Reggie barked.

Jughead feigned innocence. "Isn't it just five minutes now?"

"Try ten."

Squinting at the clock in the hallway, Jughead argued, "Sorry, Reggie. I think you're confused. It's absolutely been only five minutes. Six at the most."

"Okay, whatever." Reggie stepped out from behind the voting table. "I'm out of here."

"But wait!" Jughead shouted at his friend's back. "You have to help me carry all these boxes to the office after the voting."

"Find another sucker!" Reggie called over his shoulder.

"Well, then can you at least lend me a couple of bucks?" The plea didn't even warrant a verbal response. Reggie just waved him off. "Great." Jughead slumped back into the Ballot Master's chair. There were at least a half a dozen chocolate doughnuts left at the bake sale, waiting to be devoured—and he was stuck being Ballot Master. Jughead wailed to himself, "This is a nightmare!"

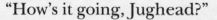

# Chapter 4

"How's it going, Jughead?"

He looked up to see that a blond purse-carrying savior had appeared before his eyes. "Betty!" he shouted. "Can you help me with these ballot boxes and lend me five dollars?"

Betty gave him an apologetic smile. "I'm sorry, Jughead. I don't have any money on me at all, and I can't help with the ballot boxes because I'm on the ballot."

"You're kidding." Jughead's face fell. "You don't have any money on you at all?"

"Not a cent."

"How are the elections going?" Veronica asked, joining them in the hallway.

"Hey, Veronica," Jughead said, swinging

27

around on her. "Your father's Mr. Money Bags. Can you lend me five dollars?"

Veronica rolled her eyes. "Well, only 'cause you asked so nice." She delved into her designer purse and pulled out her wallet. "Let's see . . . um . . . hmmm . . ." She looked up. "Can you take a credit card?"

"No." Jughead shook his head. "I don't think the bake sale takes credit cards."

"You know," Veronica went on, "I lent Archie ten dollars this morning so he could get some lunch. I bet you he still has change."

"Archie?" Jughead lit up. "He'll lend me some money. But where is he?"

Betty piped up with, "I saw him near the science lab a few minutes ago. I think he's trying to get some extra credit."

"Science lab. Got it," Jughead said, quickly trying to devise a plan. "Let's see. Voting's just about to end. Veronica, will you help me get these ballot boxes to the office?"

"Um." Veronica looked at the boxes and then at her silk blouse. She had a feeling the two shouldn't go together.

"She can't," Betty informed him. "She's on the ballot, too. It's against the rules, and neither one of us wants to be disqualified."

Jughead groaned. "Okay, can you at least keep an eye on some of the ballot boxes while I get these others to the office?"

"Sure," Betty told him. "I mean, I seriously don't think anybody is going to try to mess with the boxes."

"Great!"

A few last people slipped their votes into various boxes, and the election was over. Jughead gathered up six of the boxes and started loping toward the office.

All of a sudden—*wham!*—Jughead collided with something in the hallway. The boxes went flying, and Jughead went sprawling. "Ouch!" a female voice cried out in pain.

"What happened?" Jughead asked, staggering to his feet. Among the boxes, he saw Brigitte Reilly lying on the ground. "Brigitte! Are you okay?" He knew he should fight his impulse to yank her to her feet in case she was really hurt, so instead he just crouched down by her side to check that she was all right. "I'm so sorry. I didn't see you."

"And you didn't hear me, either." Brigitte groaned, rubbing her hip. "I called out to you, but that just seemed to make you head right for me."

"I'm so, so, so sorry," Jughead insisted. "Are you hurt? Do you need me to get you some ice or the nurse or anything?"

"No, that's okay." Brigitte gathered her legs under her to stand. "Why were you in such a hurry?"

Jughead put his arm around her waist and gently helped her to her feet. "I've got to get these boxes to the office and then find Archie to borrow some money and then go buy some doughnuts at the bake sale, which is closing in, like, seven minutes." He stopped to draw a breath. "Say, I don't suppose you could lend me a couple of bucks?"

"Sorry, Jughead." Brigitte gave him an apologetic smile. "I don't let guys crash into me and then borrow money." She looked around at the boxes on the floor. "But I will help you pick up this stuff. What are they, anyway?"

"They're the ballot boxes for the school election. I'm pretty lucky none of the boxes spilled. Then I'd really miss the bake sale."

"Uh-oh," Brigitte said.

Jughead cringed. "I don't like that sound. What's wrong?"

"The labels fell off two of the boxes," she told him. "I don't know which one goes on which."

"Oh." Jughead looked down at the two labels. One read SCHOOL PAPER and the other read FASHION SHOW. "Um . . ." He looked at the two blank boxes. "I think this one goes on this box," he said, tentatively sticking the label to the top. "And this must go on the other."

Brigitte shook her head. "How can you be sure?"

Shrugging, Jughead said, "I'm pretty sure. Besides, the office can figure it out."

"If you say so." Brigitte handed him the rest of the boxes.

Jughead glanced at a clock in the hallway.

There were only five minutes left until the end of the bake sale. "Sorry about running you over, Brigitte, but I've got to go." With that, he dashed off down the hall.

Careening into the school's office, Jughead shoved the boxes toward Ms. Phlips, the school secretary. "Here!" he shouted. "These are from the school election."

"Don't even think you're going to dump those ballot boxes on me, Jughead Jones," she snapped at him. "Those have to be officially delivered to Mr. Weatherbee."

Exasperated, Jughead swooped the boxes off the secretary's desk and hurried toward the principal's office. "Mr. Weatherbee?" he called, rapping on the door. "I have the ballot boxes."

"Come in," called a friendly voice.

Jughead flung open the door and charged into the office. "These are from the election. Where do you want them?"

"On the table by the window should be fine," the principal said, getting to his feet. "Wait a minute. There should be eight boxes."

"I know," Jughead said, panting. "I couldn't carry them all. I'll be right back with the last two." What he didn't tell the principal was that he was planning to make a short detour to the science lab.

"You didn't leave the boxes unattended, did you?" the principal asked, concern registering in his voice.

"No, of course not." Jughead tried to act like the mere idea was absurd.

"Well, bring them back here immediately," Mr. Weatherbee said in his strictest administrator's voice. "We don't want any tampering with school voting."

There were only three minutes left until the bake sale was over and the opportunity for delicious chocolate doughnuts would disappear. Jughead's heart was beating wildly in his chest. "I'm on it!" he shouted, madly dashing for the door.

The principal looked after him, impressed. "Well." He chuckled to himself. "I guess I really motivated the boy."

Jughead flung himself down the hall,

briefly stalling as he decided between the science lab or returning for the ballot boxes. But the call of the chocolate doughnuts was too strong. He sprinted for the lab. "Archie?!" he called, flinging open the door.

Dilton Doily looked up from where he was hunched over several bubbling beakers. "He's not here, Jughead."

"Well, where is he?"

Dilton shoved his glasses back up to the bridge of his nose. "I don't know. He just left. I'm sure he's still on school grounds somewhere."

"Thanks!" Jughead took off, tearing down the hall. It was only after he was twenty steps from the science lab that he thought maybe he could have asked Dilton for the money. But he had a momentum going, and it was too late to turn around. Only one minute left until the end of the bake sale, and Jughead was running out of steam. He'd run farther in the last ten minutes than he had in the last ten days. Finally, he had to slow to a jog and then to a walk.

The clock ticked forward another minute. Jughead let his shoulders sag.

The bake sale was over.

Jughead dragged himself back to the voting booth, his head hanging so low he was staring at his shoes. "Hey, Jughead! How's it going?"

Looking up, Jughead caught sight of red hair and a smiling face. His brow furrowing, he exclaimed, "Archie! What are you doing here? Why aren't you in the science lab?"

"Uh." Archie was caught by surprise. He glanced furtively at Betty and Veronica. "I finished up my extra credit and thought I'd see how the voting was going."

"Oh . . . ," Jughead groused. "It's going horribly."

"Well, then this should cheer you up. I was going by the library, and I saw there was a bake sale." Archie pulled a stack of three chocolate doughnuts out from behind his back. "I thought you might miss it because you were helping out with the elections, so I picked you up a few."

"You're kidding!" Jughead straightened up, the sight of the doughnuts dancing in his pupils. "Thanks!"

"Jughead," Betty interjected, "don't you have to deliver these two final ballot boxes?"

"Oh yeah," Jughead replied, his mouth full of chocolaty goodness. "I almost forgot."

"Come on," Archie said, picking up one of the boxes. "I'll help you get these delivered so we can get out of here."

"Thanks." Jughead's voice was muffled as he took another giant bite of doughnut. He hoisted the other box.

"Hey, you guys. Betty and I were thinking of heading over to Pop's Chocklit Shoppe for some sodas," Veronica called after them. "Do you want to meet us there?"

Archie flashed the girls a big, goofy smile. "Sure! What do you think, Jughead?"

"Definitely," his friend agreed as he polished off doughnut number one and started in on doughnut number two. "I'm starving!"

Mr. Weatherbee was starting to wonder what had happened to Jughead, so it was a relief to see him show up with the Andrews boy and the last two ballot boxes. "Here you go, Mr. Weatherbee," Jughead said, licking chocolate glaze from his lips.

"I see you felt it was necessary to stop for a snack, Jughead Jones." The principal was not pleased to have been kept waiting.

"I'm a growing boy." Jughead patted his stomach. "I've got to keep my body fueled."

This comment caused Archie to laugh. "The way you eat, you've got enough fuel for a space launch."

The principal gave both students a flat look over the top of his glasses. Then, deciding it was a battle he couldn't win, he simply said, "Just put those boxes with the other ones, boys."

"Have a nice weekend, Mr. Weatherbee," Archie said cheerfully as they headed out the door. "Oh, and when do you think you'll post the election results?"

"Bright and early Monday morning."

XOXO

The following Monday, Betty couldn't wait

to get to school. She'd been thinking about the election all weekend and was superexcited to find out who would be the next editor in chief of *The Blue and Gold*. The election results were listed on two large sheets of paper, posted in the main hallway of Riverdale High. Swarms of kids crowded around the printout. Finally getting close enough to the paper to read the results, Betty squinted and wrinkled her nose. She went over the results again. Rubbing her eyes, Betty wondered if she needed glasses. She looked at the results for the third time. Nothing had changed, the results were the same. Things just plain weren't making sense.

"Hey, Betty," Veronica called over the crowd. "How'd we do? Did we win?"

"Um . . ." The blond teenager nudged her way back through the student body.

Veronica smiled at her friend, but Betty looked so strange it was a little worrisome. "Are you all right? What's going on, Betty? Who's the new editor for *The Blue and Gold*?"

"You are," Betty replied.

# Chapter 5

Veronica clapped her hands and jumped up and down. "You're the new editor?! That's fantastic!"

"No." Betty interrupted her celebration. "You don't understand. You're the new editor. And I'm the new head of the fashion show."

"I got it, too?!" Veronica's eyes grew wide with delight. "This is so great! I can't believe we both won!"

"No, no." Betty reached out to try to settle her friend. "Listen to me very carefully. According to the election results, you, Veronica Lodge, are the new editor in chief of *The Blue and Gold*. And I . . . or me . . . or whatever, am the head of the fashion show."

"But . . ." Veronica scrunched her forehead in consternation. "That doesn't even make sense."

"I know," Betty agreed. "Something must have gotten really mixed up during the elections. I hope this isn't going to be a problem."

"Well, it can't be that hard to fix. I mean, no one's going to think we did this on purpose or anything. Are they?"

XOXO

Ginger Lopez narrowed her eyes and glared at the election results posted on the wall. "Oh, I see," she growled to herself. "So Ms. Goody-Two-Shoes, Betty Cooper, is the head of the fashion show. I would definitely list that as a fashion don't. And Ms. Charge-It-to-Daddy, Veronica Lodge, is going to be editor of the newspaper. Isn't this all just too convenient, seeing that I saw them both standing by the unattended ballot boxes after the polls had closed. Smells to me like a couple of friends have been cheating their way into office." She turned on her heel and stormed off down the hall toward the principal's office. "Not if I have anything to say about it."

XOXO

Ms. Phlips looked somewhat perturbed when Betty and Veronica entered the office. "Good morning." Betty smiled. "We need to speak to Principal Weatherbee, please."

"Pertaining to?" the secretary asked.

"Huh?"

"Why do you wish to speak to him?"

"Oh." Betty was caught a little off guard. Ms. Phlips was usually friendlier. "It's about the outcome of the school elections."

"Not another one," Ms. Phlips grumbled to herself.

"Pardon?"

"I said, there's already someone in there speaking to Principal Weatherbee about the elections," the secretary clarified.

Betty and Veronica exchanged looks. "Maybe we're not the only winners who got switched," Betty whispered to her friend. Then, looking at the secretary, she said, "I think something went wrong with the election, and we're all probably having the same problem. Do you think it would be okay if we went in?"

It was a little surprising to have students complaining about the election results, but Ms. Phlips figured the principal would probably prefer to get everything over at once. "Go on in." She nodded toward the principal's closed door.

Both girls paused outside the door, feeling awkward about walking in on someone. "I wonder who's in there." Betty reached tentatively toward the doorknob.

Veronica shrugged. "Probably someone else who won the wrong election. Now they're captain of the football team when they wanted to chair the chess club." She nodded toward the door. "Come on. Let's go in."

"But Betty and Veronica cheated!" Ginger was leaning over Mr. Weatherbee's desk and using an overly loud voice for someone speaking to the school principal. It was an unfortunate moment to have walked into the room. Both Betty and Veronica felt their faces become hot with embarrassment.

"Uh . . . ," Betty stammered.

"Whah . . . ?" Veronica contributed to the conversation.

Principal Weatherbee sighed. "Girls, this involves both of you, so you'd better come in."

Veronica found her words first. "What's going on?" she asked, stepping fully into the room.

"Well, Ms. Lopez here is a little disappointed with the election results."

"That's why we're here, too," Betty told him.

"Oh, so you've come to confess?" Ginger hissed at her.

Betty gave her a concerned look. "Are you okay, Ginger? What are you talking about?"

"You cheated on the election!" Ginger flat-out accused her. "You both did! That's how you both won!"

"We didn't cheat!" Veronica fired right back.

"Yeah, right!" Ginger swung around to face Mr. Weatherbee. "I saw them in the hallway just standing there with two of the election boxes. They could have tampered with the results at any time."

"We were watching them for Jughead!" Betty cried with outrage.

"That's right!" Veronica was quick to add. "Archie was there with us. He can vouch for us. We didn't do anything."

"Yeah, right," Ginger sneered. "Like he wouldn't lie for you." She shot Veronica daggers with her eyes.

"Hey! That's uncalled for!" Betty leaped to the defense of her friend.

"Ladies! Please!" Mr. Weatherbee thumped his desk. "Be quiet!" The girls immediately fell silent, so the principal continued. "Ms. Cooper, Ms. Lodge, why are you here?"

"It's about the election results," Betty began. "You see, I won for heading up the fashion show—"

"Don't you get it?!" Ginger interrupted, glaring at Mr. Weatherbee. "There's no way that's possible!"

"Silence," Mr. Weatherbee said in a firm whisper. Then he turned his attention back to Betty. "Go on, Ms. Cooper."

"Well, the confusing thing is that Veronica won for editor of *The Blue and Gold*, which doesn't even make sense because she wasn't running for that, she was running to head the fashion show."

"See!" Ginger cried. "She admits it! She even admits it!"

"Ms. Lopez! Do you really want a week of detention that badly?" Mr. Weatherbee asked in his best no-nonsense principal voice.

"No," she replied meekly, but her eyes were blazing.

"Anyway," Betty went on. "We think there's been some kind of mix-up with the ballots or something, because I was supposed to be the editor for the paper and Veronica was supposed to run the fashion show."

"Oh, it was just a foregone conclusion, was it?" Ginger was obviously so mad she couldn't contain herself. "You knew you were going to be the editor because you fixed the election!"

"That's a lie!" Veronica shouted. "You take that back right now! Betty would never cheat on anything, and I wouldn't, either! We're just trying to explain that there's been some kind of mistake!"

Mr. Weatherbee felt a headache taking a strong hold behind his left eyeball. The girls' voices were so shrill and so forceful. He highly doubted anyone had cheated on anything doing with the election. Ms. Lopez was obviously just being a sore loser. A sore loser with a strong vocal capacity. And as for Betty and Veronica, students at Riverdale were always committing to something, realizing it was a lot of hard work, and then trying to squirm out of it. That was nothing new. They just weren't usually quite this determined to squirm free.

While the principal was massaging his temples, the girls had squared off and were bickering at full volume. The principal felt his eyeball starting to twitch. He knew he couldn't take much more. "Be quiet!" he finally thundered.

Now, Mr. Weatherbee was an excellent principal and very fair-minded. But there are some days when even a top-notch administrator just wants the overly excited teenagers in his office to pipe down and simply accept the consequences of their actions. This was one of those days. "Ms. Lopez," he began. "You lost the election. I know you're disappointed, but you're a very bright young lady, and I'm sure there are numerous other areas where you can apply yourself and succeed."

"But . . ." Ginger tried to protest, but she could see by the look in the principal's eyes that her words would be futile.

"Ms. Cooper, Ms. Lodge, you ran for office and you won. You must accept responsibility for your actions."

"But . . ." Veronica tried, but there was no getting a word in edgewise.

"I don't want to hear one more word about this!" Mr. Weatherbee said in a stentorian voice. "Now go to your first classes and do what this institution is actually set up for you to do. Learn something!" He had thought he'd made himself clear, but the girls didn't move. They all just stood there, staring at him in disbelief. "Now!" he added. The young ladies hurried toward the door. Betty and Veronica glanced at each other, but there was no time for further discussion. The tardy bell was about to ring.

XOXO

"So," Veronica said, setting her lunch down on the table next to Betty's. "You know, I've never heard Mr. Weatherbee be quite that . . . um . . . forceful."

"I know." Betty pulled a sandwich out of a brown paper bag. "Maybe he was having a bad day or something."

"I just wish Ginger hadn't been there so we could explain. She kept interrupting, and I don't think Mr. Weatherbee really understood what we were trying to tell him."

Betty gave a small, rueful chuckle. "I know, but I sure don't want to go back and try to clear things up."

Veronica used her fork to spear a tomato out of her chopped salad. "What are we going to do?"

"Well . . ." Betty had been giving the problem a lot of thought. "I suppose I could show you about the paper. Walk you through it. Help you with articles, layouts, things like that. You know, just kind of coach you."

This suggestion made Veronica brighten slightly. "And I could sooo help you with the fashion show. You know, picking a theme, coordinating with vendors, choosing models, that kind of stuff."

"Oh, this is great." Betty felt the first signs of relief since seeing her name listed as the head of the fashion show committee that morning. "By helping each other out, we both get to enjoy the thing we really wanted to do and get a new experience and be a good friend."

"Well, I hope you plan on being an extra good friend because I don't know the first thing about being the editor of a newspaper. Even a high school newspaper," Veronica confessed.

"I could say the same to you." Betty smiled. "Sure, I can pick shoes to match a dress, but how do you put together an entire fashion show?"

Veronica smiled back and gave her best friend a wink. "Leave it to me."

At the table next to theirs, Ginger Lopez was listening to their entire conversation with eager ears. "So neither one of you knows what you're doing, huh?" she whispered under her breath. "I think you two are going to learn that being an editor and running a fashion show are much more challenging than you ever imagined." She smiled secretly to herself. "Leave it to me."

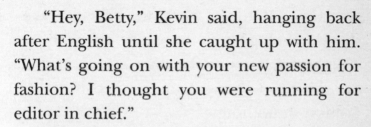

# Chapter 6

"Hey, Betty," Kevin said, hanging back after English until she caught up with him. "What's going on with your new passion for fashion? I thought you were running for editor in chief."

"So did I, but something must have gone haywire with the elections because now I'm apparently in charge of the fashion show."

Kevin frowned. "That doesn't even make sense."

"I know," Betty agreed as they started walking down the hall together. "We tried talking to Mr. Weatherbee about it, but he just said we had to learn to accept responsibility for our actions."

"Really?" Kevin was surprised. Mr. Weatherbee was usually a pretty rational man. "Maybe I should try explaining it to him. I mean, he might see that there's a problem more clearly if it came from an outside source."

"That would be great," Betty said, pausing before turning to go into her math class. "I really appreciate it."

XOXO

"Hey, Ronnie," Archie called, taking a few jogging steps to catch up with her. "Congratulations on landing editor in chief, but, uh . . . I thought you wanted to do that fashion show thingy."

Veronica rolled her eyes. "I did want to do that fashion show thingy, but something must have gone kerflooey with that election dealio because now I'm supposed to be all news-o-rama."

Archie laughed and nudged her shoulder. "Sorry. What I meant to say was, what happened with the election?"

Shaking her head, Veronica told him, "I have no idea. Betty and I tried to talk to

Mr. Weatherbee about the mix-up, but he practically threw us out of his office."

"Really?" Archie was surprised. "Old Weatherbottom gave you the boot?"

"He was totally unreasonable. And I was so looking forward to running the fashion show." Veronica pouted.

"Well, why don't you let lover boy here try talking to him?" Archie puffed up his chest. "Weatherbee and I have a special relationship."

"Oh, Archiekins! Would you?" Veronica clapped her hands together. "That would really mean a lot to me."

XOXO

"Hey, Kevin," Archie greeted his friend as they both headed toward the school's office. "Have you been sent to the principal's office?" he joked.

"No, I told Betty I'd swing by and try to work out this mix-up with the elections."

"No kidding?" Archie said with surprise. "I told Ronnie the same thing. That's why I'm here. I guess Mr. Weatherbee is being kind of a grouch about the whole thing."

"Well, maybe we should talk to him together," Kevin suggested. "I mean, if we both explain, then it might make better sense to him."

"Good idea," Archie replied as they approached Ms. Phlips's desk.

"Hi, Ms. Phlips. We're here to talk to Mr. Weatherbee," Archie told her.

The secretary stopped typing and sighed. "Let me guess. Is this about the school elections?"

"Um . . . yeah. As a matter of fact, it is." Archie cocked his head to one side. "How did you know?"

"Because there have been about a dozen kids in here before you," Ms. Phlips said. "All outraged. All complaining. All annoying. Ginger Lopez alone has caused a minimum of three scenes in this office and currently has a detention. If she comes back again, it's going to be upgraded to a Saturday detention."

"Oh . . . ," said Archie.

"Uh . . . ," said Kevin.

"So." The secretary went back to her

typing. "Do you still want to see the principal about the school elections?"

"Well . . . ," hedged Archie.

"Ummm . . . ," mumbled Kevin.

"No, thank you," the guys said in unison. They turned in a synchronized motion, as if they'd been given the command for an about-face, and hurried from the school office.

"I don't have that much of a problem with the outcome of the school elections," Archie said. "Do you?"

"No, not really," Kevin replied. "I mean, I'm sure Veronica will make a terrific editor."

XOXO

When the last bell rang for the day, Betty and Veronica had already heard the bad news from Archie and Kevin. There was absolutely no way of getting out of their elected positions. So they agreed that they'd try to make the best of it.

"Let's start with the fashion show stuff because it'll be more fun," Veronica suggested.

Betty's face fell slightly. "The newspaper is fun."

Rethinking her words, Veronica said, "You know, that sounded really snarky. I'm sorry. What I meant to say is, can we start with the fashion show stuff because I'm really excited about it and I think it'll be fun?"

Smiling, Betty agreed, "Sounds good to me."

"Great." The two girls started walking toward the school's parking lot. "First things first," Veronica continued. "We should stop by my house for a change of wardrobe."

Betty looked down at her jean mini, scoop neck T-shirt, and mules. "What's wrong with what I'm wearing?"

"Nothing," Veronica assured her. "You look supercute. But not exactly couture."

"So?"

"When you go to a high-end boutique, you dress like you have designer fashions coming out of your ears."

Betty looked down. "But I don't have designer fashions coming out of my ears. "

"Don't worry. I have enough designer labels for both of us."

# Chapter 7

Thirty minutes later, Betty was dolled up in an outfit that cost more than her entire wardrobe combined. She sat in the passenger seat of Veronica's car and tried not to wrinkle it. "Do you want to stop at the Chocklit Shoppe first and get a soda?" Veronica asked.

"No way," Betty told her. "I'm worried I might stain something."

"Don't worry." Veronica laughed. "That's why they invented dry cleaners."

It took only a few minutes for them to zip across town in Veronica's red convertible. "Okay," she said, wheeling her car into the parking lot of a fashionable boutique. "Mary Rose has some really cute stuff in her store, and she's helped with the fashion show since we were freshmen."

Betty nodded. "Great."

A bell over the door tinkled as they entered the shop. An elegant-looking woman who smelled of lilacs greeted them. "Welcome to . . . Oh, hello, Veronica."

"Hi, Mary Rose." Veronica gave her a big smile.

"Just browsing today or are you looking for something special?"

"Well, actually, Riverdale's annual charity fashion show is coming up," Veronica explained.

"Oh, that's right. The fashion show. Is it that time of year already?"

Assuming the question was rhetorical, Veronica continued. "This is Betty Cooper. She's the head of the show this year."

"It's nice to meet you, Betty." Mary Rose extended a well-manicured hand.

"Nice to meet you," Betty replied. She was already grateful that Veronica had spiffed up her outfit. "I hope you're interested in participating in the fashion show this year."

Mary Rose thought about it a moment and then smiled. "Yes, I think I am. We don't usually get a lot of teenage clients from contributing to the fashion show, but mothers of the models sometimes swing by. I think it definitely helps my business."

"That's great," Veronica said. "We really appreciate it, Mary Rose."

"Well, I appreciate you as a customer," the boutique owner told her.

Betty got a business card and contact information, entering it all in a notebook she had labeled FASHION SHOW. After a few more minutes of small talk they were back in the car. "Well, that was easy," Betty said while cinching her seat belt. "I'm glad we've got the clothing all set up. What's next?"

Veronica squinted over at her. "What do you mean by all set up? Mary Rose was just our first stop. We have to have at least five boutiques signed on to do the show before we'll be in a good spot."

"You're kidding?" Betty wasn't sure why she was surprised, but she was. "You mean we're not done?"

"Nope." Veronica pulled the car out of the lot. "Next we're headed to Marlene's in the mall."

"So." Betty pulled her notebook out of her bag. She figured she might as well ask some questions while they were driving. "What else needs to get done for the fashion show?"

"Well, let's see." Veronica gave it some thought. "After getting the vendors, you need to decide on a theme, so the boutique owners can put together some outfits. Then there's ordering the invitations, choosing the models, fitting sessions with the models, renting a runway for the gym, lighting and a sound system, decorations, of course, some type of light refreshments." Veronica scratched her chin while Betty hurriedly scribbled in her notebook. "Publicity is important. You also have to address the invitations and get them in the mail, hire someone for hair and makeup, and you definitely want to do at least one run-through with all the models and the clothing before you have the show."

"Wow," Betty said. Her head was starting to spin. "I never realized how much work went into putting on a fashion show."

"Don't think of it as work," Veronica said, stopping at a red light. "It's fashion. It's supposed to be fun."

"Yeah, but"—Betty couldn't help but sigh a little—"I just wish, you know, it meant something more than just beautiful clothes."

"It's for charity. That's something," Veronica pointed out.

"Yeah, and that's great, but . . . I don't know, just girls in pretty clothes. It doesn't have a lot of substance. You know, like, what does it mean?"

The light changed, and Veronica stepped on the gas. She couldn't help but chuckle at her friend. Betty was always trying to make everything boring and meaningful instead of just having fun. But, realizing Betty really expected an answer, she said, "It means you have good taste."

The next afternoon the tables turned, and it was Betty's time to show Veronica around the Riverdale High newspaper office. "So tomorrow, you'll probably want to call a story meeting," Betty suggested.

"What's that?" Veronica wanted to know as she thumbed through some back issues of *The Blue and Gold*, realizing she'd never actually looked closely at the school paper.

"It's where all the writers pitch their story ideas. Then you decide what stories work for the next issue. Larry okayed a lot of the stories before he left, so you'll really just want to go over who is doing what and fill in any gaps."

Veronica raised her eyebrows. "Sounds easy. Larry's already done half the work."

"Well, it's not that easy because you have to decide what's going to be the headline story and then what other stories will go on the front page. Then you have to fill the rest of the paper. You want to choose articles that are interesting, but you can't forget to include school news, socials events, school announcements, and sports."

"Okay." Veronica wondered if she should be writing things down.

"Once you decide on a story, you have to assign a photographer to cover it. Some writers will take their own pictures, but most won't," Betty warned her.

"Got it."

"You'll want the writers to get their stories in early because you'll need time to go over each one to check for spelling and formatting errors."

Veronica made a face. "Don't the writers do that?"

"They try," Betty explained, "but they don't always catch everything. That's the editor's job."

"Great," Veronica muttered. Being an editor didn't sound like much fun. Picking stories was kind of neat, but the rest of it just sounded like correcting papers.

"Also," Betty continued, ignoring her friend's lack of enthusiasm, "you've got to remember ad sales. We need that money to keep the paper running."

"No problem," Veronica told her. "I'll just get my dad to take out a full-page ad."

Betty looked a little concerned about the idea. "What would he be advertising?"

Veronica shrugged. "Who cares?"

"Well, I care," Betty told her. "The paper means a lot to me, and I think you should pursue legitimate advertisers rather than just getting money from your dad."

Rolling her eyes, Veronica agreed. "Okay, fine. I'll get real advertisers. What else have I got to do?"

Veronica had meant to be sarcastic, but Betty took her seriously. "Okay, good. I'm glad you asked. Once you have the articles, the photos, and the ads all ready to go, then you have to work on layout."

"That seems like an awful lot of work. Isn't there a graphic designer or somebody that does all that?" Veronica yawned.

"Nope, it's all up to the editor. Kevin will probably help you. He's good at design," Betty replied. "After that, all that's left to do is printing and distribution."

Veronica felt tired just from hearing about all the effort it took to put a newspaper together. She wished she'd taken notes because she couldn't remember half of what Betty had told her. Finally, she said, "I don't know, Betty. This whole paper thing kind of feels like one gigantic homework assignment."

Betty laughed. "It's a lot of work, I'll give you that. But there's no feeling in the world more satisfying than when an issue of *The Blue and Gold* actually goes to press."

Veronica didn't say anything out loud, but she could think of about two zillion things she believed would be more satisfying. For example, finding the perfect pair of black pumps. But Betty thought the world of the paper, so she figured there had to be something to it, and she'd just learn what that was while being editor in chief. After all, being an editor was really just telling people what to do, and Veronica liked doing that. So maybe things wouldn't be so bad after all.

# Chapter 8

"Hey, Kevin," Betty called as she trotted up the steps to school the next morning.

"Good morning, Ms. Fashionista," he replied.

Giving him half a smirk, she said, "That's kind of what I wanted to talk to you about."

"What?" Kevin yanked open the door, and they both walked inside.

"Well, you know how I ended up the head of the charity fashion show?" Kevin nodded, so Betty continued. "I was kind of wondering if you wanted to help me out. I mean, Veronica's going to be my fashion spirit guide and everything, but there's a ton to do, and I want to at least try to have some fun while doing it. So . . . I was wondering if you wanted to be on the fashion show committee?" She gave him a hopeful glance.

"Betty." Kevin looked at her and smiled. "Just because I'm gay, it doesn't mean I'm into fashion shows."

Betty's face turned bright red. "But you are one of the best dressed guys in the school. And there are only girls on the committee right now, and half of them are superangry because I'm in charge and I didn't technically even run for the position. And I was thinking that it might be nice to have a friend there, who's also a guy, who's also fashionable."

They both turned and started heading toward their lockers. Kevin laughed. "Thanks a lot for complimenting my style, Betty. It's nice to be appreciated."

XOXO

In the student parking lot, Veronica and Archie were having their own conversation. "So between the articles and the layouts and getting ads and distribution, I'm going to need a lot of help."

"Oh," Archie said, noncommittally looking out the car window.

"I mean, I obviously can't do it all by myself," Veronica hinted.

"Uh-huh." Archie gave a bob of his head in agreement but still wouldn't meet her eyes.

"And, of course, whoever sells the most ads gets a free ride on the space shuttle," she said casually.

"That sounds really interesting," Archie replied, eyeing the front of the school.

"Archie!"

"What?"

"You're not even listening to me!" Veronica fumed.

"Sure I am," he assured her. "Mostly. I mean, you're going to be the editor of the paper, and it's going to be a lot of work. That's the gist of it, right?"

"The gist of it is, I'm going to need a lot of help," she said, giving him a significant look.

"I bet," Archie replied, doing his best not to take the hint. "It's a good thing you've got Betty." Then, reluctantly recognizing

Veronica was expecting more from him, he hastily added, "And I hear there are a lot of great kids on the paper. I mean, you know, hard workers and everything."

Veronica folded her arms. "Archie, do you want to help me with the paper or not?"

Blushing, Archie confessed, "I'm going to have to go with not."

This made Veronica's eyes pop. She wasn't used to her almost boyfriend being so unsupportive. "Why not?"

"Well . . ." It was time to fess up. Archie couldn't avoid it any longer. "Reggie said he was going to be one of the male models for the fashion show, and I always kind of thought that maybe I could be a male model. And the fashion show is the perfect opportunity for me to start strutting my stuff."

Veronica tried hard not to burst out laughing. She bit her lips to keep the giggles in. It really wasn't her intent to hurt Archie's feelings. After all, she found him attractive. But he wasn't exactly classically good-looking or anything. He was more of the cute, slightly geeky type with a good personality. Which was totally attractive as far as she was concerned, but his look didn't exactly scream, "Look out, New York City, here comes the next superhunk!" So she knew she had to be politic in her response. "Um . . . ," she started. "Have you talked to Betty about this? I mean, she's the one that will be signing up the models."

"Not yet, but come on." Archie did a classic muscle flex. "I've been working out."

Veronica really wanted his help with the paper, but he was acting so hopeful and cute about modeling, it just made her heart melt. She leaned over and gave him a kiss on the cheek. "Oh, Archiekins, I think you'd make a wonderful model."

XOXO

"Hey, Betty," Ginger called. Betty had decided to take her study hall in the library, and Ginger was there, sitting alone at one of the tables. "Want to join me?"

"Um, okay." Betty tentatively put her books down. "Are you sure? I mean, you seemed pretty upset that I'm in charge of the fashion show."

"Oh, that." Ginger waved off the memory. "Sorry about that. I was just disappointed I lost. I didn't mean to freak out or anything."

"Okay . . ." Betty was still hesitant.

"Relax, Betty. I'm totally over it," Ginger insisted. "In fact, I still really want to help put the show together. Seriously, I got being angry out of my system, and I'm all about helping now."

Betty smiled and slid into the chair. "That would be great! I can use all the help I can get. Especially from someone like you, who has so much experience in fashion."

Looking down in an attempt to appear humble, Ginger said, "Well, I don't have that much experience."

"Are you kidding? You write for *Sparkle Magazine*! I'm not really even into fashion, and I know that's a huge deal. What's it like, getting to go to New York all the time and meeting all those fashionable people?"

Ginger had to smile. "Well, to be honest, it is pretty awesome. And I do get a lot of inside information. You know, about what's going to be hot. It's a great way to find out what's going to be sizzling on the runways next season."

"Really?" Betty leaned forward and said in a half whisper, "So what is going to be sizzling? I mean, I have to pick a theme for the fashion show, and I really have no idea. I don't want you to reveal any trade secrets or anything, but if you could just give me a hint in the right direction."

"Okay." Ginger leaned in, conspiratorially. "I have a total scoop on what's going to be huge with a ton of designers next season. It's practically going to be the theme for every major show."

"Really?" Betty leaned closer. "What?"

Ginger scanned the room to make sure no one else was listening. "The environment."

"Huh? Are you kidding?"

"No, seriously. A lot of top designers are trying to get away from the superficiality of fashion. Do you know what I mean? Like, so you've made a taffeta dress that costs like a gazillion dollars. Big deal."

"But don't fashion designers want to sell

expensive clothing? Isn't that pretty much how they make their living?"

"Well, sure," Ginger admitted. "But, I mean, fashion doesn't just have to be shallow, you know? It can have meaning."

Betty was surprised. "It can?"

"Sure." Ginger shrugged. "I mean, just because you design couture clothes, it doesn't mean you can't be green about it. In fact, a lot of the big designers are totally concerned about the environment."

"They are?"

"Don't act so stunned."

"Yeah, but you know . . . fashion designers just seem so . . ." Betty floundered.

"Superficial?"

Betty turned a little pink. She didn't ever like to insult people. Even people she didn't know. "Well, kind of. And they also seem so . . ."

"Greedy?"

"No." Betty shook her head. "Not exactly. I was going to say . . ."

"Ruthless?" Ginger tried. "Soulless?

Completely lacking integrity?"

"No!" Betty said adamantly. "I would never say any of those things. I'm just surprised to hear that the newest trend in fashion is going to be about the environment."

Ginger started gathering her books. "Well, you can trust me, it's absolutely true. Only"—she paused for a moment, looking thoughtful—"maybe you shouldn't tell anyone I said anything. I mean, I'm happy to give you the inside info, but I'd hate to get in trouble at *Sparkle* or anything."

"Oh, I totally understand," Betty assured her. "I mean, I really appreciate your advice. And I love the idea of doing a fashion show that's about the environment."

"Yeah." Ginger smiled. "Maybe you could make that the show's theme."

Betty all but glowed. She was wondering how to make the fashion show into something she could stand behind, and this was the perfect solution. "That's a great idea!" she enthused.

"Well, don't tell anyone I said anything,"

Ginger whispered. "Feel free to take all the credit." With that, she grabbed her books and hurried out of the library.

"That was so nice of her," Betty said to herself. "I'm feeling better about the fashion show already."

# Chapter 9

No more than ten seconds after Ginger left the library, Veronica sauntered up to Betty's table. "Hey," she said, plunking down her books. "Ready to talk about a theme for the show? I was thinking romance."

"Oh." Betty looked thoughtful. "Wasn't that the theme of last year's show?"

"Not at all," Veronica informed her. "Last year, the theme was love. But a lot of people didn't get it. The show wasn't supposed to be about love between people or anything, it was supposed to be about the love of shoes."

"Well," Betty hedged, "I'm thinking we should go with something completely new, but, you know, cutting edge."

77

"Okay." Veronica sat down and pulled out a notebook. "I wrote down some other ideas." Flipping to the right page, she said, "Oh, here. You'll love this. What about the law of the jungle? Everything could be animal prints and tropical flowers."

Betty wrinkled her nose. "Not my favorite."

"Geek chic?"

"Um . . . I'm not feeling it."

"Well, fine." Veronica slammed down her notebook. "What do you think would make a good theme?"

Betty took a deep breath. "I'm thinking the show should be about the environment. You know, make it a green theme."

"Green?" Veronica said, unable to stop herself from executing an extreme eye roll. "It's a fashion show, not Earth Day."

"Yeah, I know, but just because it's fashion doesn't mean it can't be, you know, environmentally friendly," Betty tried to explain.

Veronica felt a small, burning knot in the pit of her stomach. She was megaexcited about the fashion show. It really was the most important event of the year, and if there was any justice in the world, she would be running it. And now her best friend was trying to turn it into something stupid. It was supposed to be about the true beauty that is fashion. "Betty," she said very slowly. "Not everything has to have a deep social meaning attached to it. Some things can just be about fun and a passion for clothes and stuff. It's already for charity. Isn't that enough?"

"Well, sure," Betty tried to reassure her, but what she was secretly thinking was that Veronica may be Riverdale High's most fashionable student, but she didn't have the inside scoop straight from *Sparkle Magazine*. "It's just . . . I really think being green is going to be the next huge fashion trend. I mean, just because someone's a couture designer, doesn't mean they don't care about the earth."

"Um . . . I guess that could be true." Veronica felt forced to agree, even though the core of her being raged against it. "But I think fashion designers are more about giving to green causes rather than actually making their designs environmentally friendly." The school bell rang, indicating the end of the period. Both girls got to their feet. "Okay, well, let's talk about this after school."

"But we're doing the newspaper meeting after school," Betty reminded her.

"Oh yeah. I forgot. But, come on, picking a theme for the fashion show is way important."

"Getting the next issue of *The Blue and Gold* out is important, too," Betty snapped.

"You're right. I'm sorry," Veronica said as they headed for the library exit. "Let's talk about the show after the meeting."

"Okay, fine," Betty agreed. As she hurried down the hall to her next class, she couldn't help but wonder why Veronica was so against an environmental theme. If anyone in the school should have an inkling about the coming trends in fashion, Betty assumed it would be her best friend.

XOXO

"Hi," Ginger said as Veronica strolled into her history class.

Veronica gave the girl a suspicious look. "What's going on? Are you getting ready to call me a cheater again or what?"

Ginger gave her a sheepish grin. "No, I'm over that now. And I'm sorry. I just really got excited about the paper, and I was megadisappointed I didn't win. I shouldn't have taken it out on you."

"I wish you did win," Veronica said, half to herself as she plunked down in the desk next to Ginger's. "Then I wouldn't have to exhaust myself putting the thing together."

"Don't you want to be on the paper?"

"Um, sure." Veronica rolled her eyes. "Who doesn't?"

"Well," Ginger conceded, "it is a little dry, I guess. I mean, the whole thing could probably use an overhaul, if you know what I mean."

Veronica glanced sideways at the girl. "Not really."

"I mean, it's just kind of . . ." She searched for the right word. "Old-fashioned. I mean, who actually reads the thing? That's why I wanted to be editor in chief so bad. I was going to give *The Blue and Gold* a face-lift, a tune-up, and a whole new attitude."

"What kind of attitude?" Veronica asked, but she said it quietly because the teacher was about to start class.

Ripping a piece of paper out of her notebook, Ginger scribbled something across the top, folded it, and then lobbed it onto Veronica's desk. Unfolding the note, Veronica read a single word. *Tabloid!* Sticking a question mark after it, she slipped the note back onto Ginger's desk. A few seconds later, the paper was returned. This time Ginger had added to the one word. The entire note read, "Tabloid!? Would be fabulous! Talk after class."

Veronica was usually pretty good at paying attention during history. The class was studying Attila the Hun, and she had to admit, he was a pretty fascinating guy. But Ginger's note got her brain buzzing. What if she did add a little more spice to *The Blue and Gold*? Not a full-on scandal sheet or anything like that, but a little school gossip would probably help circulation. There could also be an advice column, fashion dos and don'ts, a horoscope, all kinds of stuff. In fact, the more Veronica thought about it, the more excited she became. She was the editor in chief, after all. There was no reason she had to stick with the same old boring format *The Blue and Gold* had been doing since 1942. She could be an innovator and remake the whole paper.

By the time the bell rang, signaling the end of history class, Veronica's head was full of ideas. Ginger caught up with her in the hallway. "So," Ginger began, "like I was saying about, you know, pepping up the paper a little bit."

"Oh, I think making the paper more like a tabloid is an awesome idea!" Veronica enthused.

"You do?" Ginger seemed a little surprised.

"Definitely! I mean, why stick with fussy and boring?"

"That's my point exactly," Ginger told her.

"I really can't thank you enough, Ginger. I mean, I was really floundering, trying to figure out what to do with the paper, and then you're here with such a genius idea. There could be an advice column and something on fashion and even a little gossip just about who's dating who," Veronica gushed. "The paper's going to be great! You really saved me!"

"Oh, don't even think of giving me the credit," Ginger urged her. "I just had the tabloid idea, but it sounds like you've really taken off with it. I don't even feel like it's my idea anymore. All of the credit should go to you."

"No! Really?"

"I insist," Ginger told her. "The paper is your baby now. You've got to run with it."

"Wow! That's so nice of you. I really appreciate it."

"It's my pleasure." Ginger gave her a tight, little smile. "Seriously, don't ever mention it."

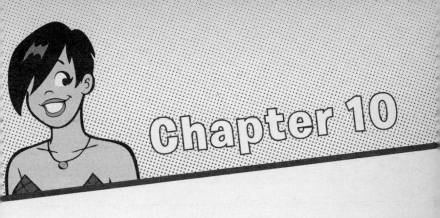

# Chapter 10

Veronica was more excited for her first newspaper meeting as editor in chief than she could have imagined. Sure, half *The Blue and Gold* staff was furious that she was in charge, but most of them had voiced their grievances to Principal Weatherbee and had been shut down.

There was no way around it. If they wanted to keep working on the paper, then they had to accept that Veronica was in charge. Even so, she was glad Betty would be there with her to smooth the way.

She really would have preferred running the fashion show, but she figured she might as well make the best of it. And now that she had her tabloid idea, the prospect of working on the paper seemed a lot brighter.

"Ready to guide me through the rough waters of my first newspaper meeting?" she asked, sliding up to Betty's locker at the end of the day.

"You know it." Betty smiled. "Some of the kids were a little grumpy at first, but I think everything is going to be fine. And besides, like I said, Larry assigned a lot of the stories before he left. There isn't a ton for you to do at the moment."

"I think things are going to be better than fine. I came up with some really cool ideas to update *The Blue and Gold*."

Betty closed her locker and cocked an eyebrow at her friend. "Really? Like what?"

Together they headed down the hall toward the newspaper office. "Well, first of all, I think it might be fun to have a fashion column. You know, tips on what to wear and what's totally out of style."

"Oh." Betty thought about it. "That might be good . . . I mean, as long as it was positive and not being too judgmental or mean to anyone."

Veronica restrained herself from rolling her eyes. Betty was always concerned about everybody's feelings, which was great, but sometimes she took it a bit too far. "Okay, point taken. I was also thinking—" But before she could continue, Kevin Keller tugged on her sleeve.

"There you guys are. Everybody's waiting for the first official staff meeting with Ronnie in charge. Get a move on." He dashed off down the hall.

"I guess we'd better get in there," Betty said, increasing her pace. "But I really want to hear your other ideas."

Veronica shrugged. "I guess you can hear them when everyone else does. Let's go."

Kevin, Chuck, Nancy, Ginger, and about a dozen other students were sitting around the newspaper office, chatting. Everyone fell silent as soon as Betty and Veronica walked in the room. Veronica could practically feel the stink eye from half the room. Betty must have felt it, too, because she immediately said, "Come on, guys. Don't look so sour. Everything's going to be fine. In fact, everything's going to be great. Veronica's going to bring some fresh ideas to the paper, and I'm sure these last two issues of the year are going to be two of the best." People loosened up a little and appeared to be slightly more receptive, so Betty turned to Veronica and said, "Okay, you're in charge. Let's hear your idea."

"Thanks, Betty." Veronica stepped forward. "Um, I know this is a little weird because of the voting mix-up, but as most of you have figured out, Mr. Weatherbee is being absolutely stubborn about it." Everyone nodded in agreement, so she continued. "At first I was kind of freaked out about it, too, but then I figured I might as well make the best out of it. And then the more I thought about it, the more I got excited about breathing some new life into *The Blue and Gold*."

"Uh, excuse me," Alison Adams called from the back of the room. "Just what exactly was wrong with *The Blue and Gold*'s old life? I mean, I thought some of the issues we put out this year were pretty good."

"That's right," Kim Wong added, brushing her straight black hair out of her eyes. "So you've never worked on the paper, but you have a problem with what we're doing?"

"No, that's not what I said," Veronica replied, feeling a bit flustered. "I just meant that sometimes a little change is good, and maybe if we give the paper a face-lift, we can improve ad sales and increase readership."

Kim folded her arms. "I think things are pretty fine the way they are right now. There's no reason to change anything."

"Yeah," Alison added.

"Hold up, ladies." Kevin lifted both of his hands in a placating gesture. "Let's just hear what Veronica has to say. Maybe she has some good ideas." He turned to face her. "Go ahead, Ronnie."

"Okay," she said a bit hesitantly. "My first idea is that we make the paper a little more topical. Just some light gossip, like who's dating who and where people are going on their summer vacations. If they're going someplace cool, of course. That kind of thing." No one said anything so she kept going. "And I thought maybe we could have an advice column, if students wanted to write in. Also, like, horoscopes maybe and a style column and . . ." She drifted off. The stares from the writers were not receptive. Not receptive at all.

# Chapter 11

There were several long seconds of silence, and then Alison jumped to her feet. "Are you crazy? You want to turn *The Blue and Gold* into some trashy scandal magazine!"

"No!" Veronica protested. "I don't want to make it a scandal magazine. I just want to drag it into the twenty-first century. You know, make it something people might actually want to read."

"Plenty of people read *The Blue and Gold*!" Kim joined the fight.

"Oh yeah?" Veronica put her hands on her hips defiantly. "Name three. And you can't count anyone that actually works on the paper."

That stalled Kim for the moment, but Alison was furious. "I knew this would happen! I knew it! We take a lot of pride in our school paper, and now you just want to come in and ruin it! You weren't even elected to be editor in chief!"

On some level, Veronica knew Kim was right. She wasn't elected editor in chief, and she knew next to nothing about the paper. Still, she thought her ideas were really good, and her ego felt a little scorched that Kim rejected them so severely. Unfortunately, she let that part of her brain get the best of her. "But I *am* editor in chief!" Veronica shouted right back.

"Veronica." Kim lowered her voice, but held firm. "Either I get to do my article about the school's dress code, which was approved by Larry before he left, or I'm walking."

Veronica folded her arms and nodded toward the exit. Kim was out the door like a shot with Alison hard on her heels. "Anyone else?" she asked. Two guys got up and nervously shuffled out of the room. Nancy got to her feet, but Chuck stayed where he was. "Sorry, honey, but I need the experience of having my comics in print," he explained. Then, after glancing apprehensively in Veronica's direction, he added in a lower voice, "No matter how bad the paper turns out to be."

"B-b-b-ut," Nancy stuttered, "this is something we were supposed to do together."

"Then stay here and do it with me." He gave her a broad grin, his teeth looking extra white in contrast with his cocoa-colored skin.

Nancy had a moment of mental conflict and then sat back down. "Oh, all right," she capitulated. "Veronica," she called across the room, "if you're serious about this change, I'll do the horoscopes. But I want to do the article that Larry and I agreed on, too."

"Fantastic," Veronica said, feeling a small wave of relief. Not everyone was going to immediately stomp out the door. It didn't really matter if she took in a few boring articles along with the new ones. She could always pull any extra articles she didn't feel like using when it was time to go to press.

Veronica took a sideways glance at Betty and then wished she hadn't. Her best friend's face was the bright red of anger. There was practically steam coming out of her ears. "Uh-oh," Veronica whispered under her breath. Betty was obviously not thrilled with the new direction in which the editor in chief had decided to steer *The Blue and Gold.*

"Ronnie," Betty said through clenched teeth, "can I speak to you in private for a minute?" She grabbed her best friend by the wrist and practically dragged her into the hall. "What are you doing?" she demanded in a loud hiss as soon as she had yanked shut the door to the newspaper office.

Wrenching her hand out of Betty's iron grip, Veronica said, "I'm updating the paper. Just like I said."

"You're not updating it. You're giving it a total overhaul."

Veronica shrugged. "I'm just trying to do what I think it needs to make it actually successful."

"It is successful!" Betty fumed.

"I mean successful with people who aren't total geeks."

Betty took a few steps backward. "Is that what this is about? You think the paper isn't cool enough for you to be a part of it?"

"Um . . ." Veronica hedged.

"I see. So rather than learn what it's all about, you want to just change it all to suit your tastes?"

"Well . . ."

Betty glared at her friend, her hands on her hips. "Listen, I know you'd rather do something superficial, like run the fashion show, but you're editor in chief, and it would be nice if you didn't ruin the paper for the rest of us."

"Why do you even care?" Veronica fired back. "You'll be too busy ruining the fashion show to worry about me transforming the paper into something cool people will actually want to read."

"I assume by *cool* you actually mean *shallow*."

"Listen, Betty, the fashion show is for

charity. It at least does some good for people instead of bore them to sleep."

"Which charity?" Betty snarled.

Veronica was thrown for a moment. She honestly didn't know which charity the show was supporting. That part had never interested her, so she had never bothered to ask. "I . . . ," she floundered. "Well . . . that doesn't matter. No one's going to get any money with you in charge. How can you possibly think people are going to want to go to a fashion show about recycling?"

"It's for the children's hospital! Which does matter. A lot. And besides, I never said the theme was going to be about recycling. I said I wanted it to be about the environment."

"It can't be about the environment. That's the stupidest idea I've ever heard!" Veronica was practically shouting.

"You know, Veronica, you're not the last word in fashion."

Veronica let out a derisive snort. "I am in this town!"

"You're not the only one who knows about

fashion in Riverdale," Betty told her. "Not even close."

"Oh." Veronica folded her arms and cocked her head to the side. "And I suppose you think you've got the four-one-one on fashion."

Betty mimicked her, also folding her arms and cocking her head. "I know enough to know that the environment is a great theme for the fashion show."

"Listen, Betty, I'm not helping you if you insist on keeping that stupid theme."

"Fine." Betty stuck her chin up in the air. "I don't need your help, anyway. The green theme stays."

"Good luck with that," Veronica scoffed.

"Well, good luck destroying the paper. I suppose you don't need my help to make it a total disaster."

Veronica narrowed her eyes. "I'm sure I'll do just fine without you. Consider yourself cut from the staff."

Betty was shocked. She loved the paper. She really hadn't expected that Veronica would go that far. Her nose began to burn, and she blinked rapidly, trying to keep back the tears that were filling her eyes. "Fine!" She turned and stormed off down the hall.

"Fine," Veronica said, spinning around and wrenching open the door to the newspaper office.

Several students stumbled back from where they had been listening at the door. Kevin walked over and hooked his arm around her shoulder. "Don't worry about it, Ronnie. A lot of people don't like change, but I think you're an innovator."

Veronica gave him a thin smile and then turned to the paper's staff. "Okay, everyone, let's get this meeting started. We can keep some of the articles Larry assigned, but we need to get some fresh stuff in there, too."

Ginger smiled gleefully to herself as she crossed the room to grab an empty seat. "Fine."

# Chapter 12

"Dilton, wait up," Betty called as Dilton Doily, aka Riverdale High's science super genius, was about to enter the science lab.

"Hi, Betty." Dilton waited for her, adjusting his glasses.

It was the day after Betty and Veronica's big fight, and both girls were still pretty steamed. Betty knew she had to press forward with the fashion show, even without Veronica's help.

Smiling, she took a deep breath and said, "Well, I don't know if you've heard, but I'm the head of the charity fashion show."

Dilton snuffled, "I think everyone in the entire school knows that."

"Okay, good." Betty was a bit surprised, but

only because Dilton always seemed to have his nose buried in a book when he wasn't in the lab. "Anyway, I was wondering if you would like to be one of the models for the show?"

Catching his glasses from falling off his face, Dilton did a double take. "Me? You want me to be in the fashion show?"

"Sure," Betty told him. "I think you'd make a great model."

"But, Betty," he leaned in and said in a low voice as if he were worried someone might overhear them. "I don't know if you realize this, but I'm a bona fide science geek."

"So?"

"So geeks don't usually get invited to strut around on a catwalk."

"Don't be ridiculous, Dilton." Betty laughed. "The nerd look is a great look, and it's superhot right now. I definitely want you to be part of the show."

"Well"—the bona fide science geek blushed a little—"if it'll help you out, I guess I could be one of your models."

"That's great, Dilton!" Betty couldn't stop

herself from giving him a hug, which made him blush even more. "I'll keep you updated about when we're doing fittings and run-throughs and stuff."

As Dilton ducked into the science lab, Archie and Reggie came lumbering down the hall. "Hey, Betty," they both called, hurrying toward her.

"Hi, guys. What's up?"

"When are you going to start picking models for the fashion show?" Archie asked.

"Now," Betty told them. "I just asked Dilton if he'd like to be a model."

"Dilton?" Reggie said, doing little to conceal his surprise. "Why'd you ask Dilton?"

Betty narrowed her eyes, suspicious of Reggie's tone. "Because I think he's got a good look."

"Well, if you want good-looking, search no further." Reggie gave her a rakish grin. "Go ahead and book me. I'll be in your show."

"We both will be," Archie said, shoving Reggie aside a little.

"Really? That'd be great." Betty pulled out

a notebook and wrote down both their names.

"I could be your featured model," Reggie said, stepping in front of Archie. "I'm lean, I'm fit, and I'm ready for the catwalk."

"Or feature me," Archie said, elbowing his competition out of the way. "After all"—he ran his hand through his bright red hair—"red really stands out under the lights."

"You're puny," Reggie said, elbowing him right back. "Betty needs someone with stage presence."

"I am not puny." Archie flexed a bicep. "I've been working out twice a week."

"Well, I've been working out three times a week," Reggie fired back, flexing his own muscles.

"Well, I'm going to the gym right now," Archie insisted.

"Not if I get there first," Reggie said, giving his friend a shove and then sprinting down the hall. Archie was hot on his heels.

"Okay, well, I've got the two of you signed up!" Betty called after them.

Hurrying into the library, Betty saw

Ginger, Nancy, Midge Klump, Ethel Muggs, and Brigitte Reilly all gathered around a big table. "Oh good, you're all here." She smiled as she walked over to them.

"What's up, Betty?" Midge asked.

"Well, it's about the fashion show. I need models, and I'm hoping you girls will help me out." Some of the girls smiled, some turned red, and some whispered to one another. Some did all three. Midge was the first to speak. "Yeah, um . . . Betty? My name's Midge, not Mammoth."

"I know who you are, Midge." Betty smiled at her. "So?"

"I'm five foot nothing. Not exactly your classic model type."

Betty crossed her arms. "Don't you think nonstatuesque people buy clothes?"

"Sure." Midge was confused. "I guess they do. I mean, yeah. We do."

"Well, then why can't there be models that come in different sizes? I mean, different clothes look good on different people."

Midge broke out into a grin. "Yeah, you

know what? Count me in. I always thought it might be fun to get on the runway."

The other girls agreed and quickly signed up to be models. All but one. Brigitte Reilly hung back and waited for the other girls to leave. "What's going on, Brigitte?" Betty asked once the coast was clear. "Don't you want to be part of the show?"

"Sure I do," Brigitte said, even though she looked miserable about it.

"So then what's the holdup?"

Brigitte patted her stomach, which was slightly fuller than the other girls that had been asked to be models. "This," she said, not meeting Betty's eyes. "People might not mind a short model, but they sure will notice a heavy one."

"First of all, you're not that heavy," Betty told her. "It's just a few extra pounds. And secondly, fashion should be for everyone, not just the domain of skeletonlike supermodels."

"I guess." Brigitte shrugged.

"What if I promise that all your outfits will be really, really flattering, and that we'll bring in a professional to do everyone's hair and makeup? Would that make you a little more interested in doing the show?"

Brigitte didn't look convinced, but she did look like she might be persuaded. "There are so many skinny girls in this school. Why not ask one of them?"

"Because they're not you, and I think you'd make a great model. You've got good hair and great skin. And I like the way you carry yourself when you walk. You don't just stump along, you kind of float."

The last comment made Brigitte blush. "Well, I did take a lot of ballet when I was little."

"So will you do it?" Betty asked her. "Please, please, pretty please? I promise you'll look fabulous, and it'll be superfun."

"Okay." Brigitte gave a shy smile. "Sign me up."

Meanwhile, Veronica was in the newspaper office with Kevin, her unofficial assistant editor. "So Nancy's doing the horoscope and some boring article about hygiene in the cafeteria. We might have to cut that. I don't know what can be done to make that kind of story interesting."

"You could change it to an undercover investigation about what really goes into the sloppy joes," Kevin suggested.

Veronica laughed. "That might actually work." Then, looking at her notes, she went on. "Ginger's doing something about whether the school should push to use more recycled paper. Why is everyone so focused on the environment lately? It's weird."

"Well . . ." Kevin gave it some thought. "A lot of people think about the environment the way you think about your favorite pair of shoes. You want to keep them for a really long time, so you have to make sure to take good care of them."

Rolling her eyes, Veronica laughed. "Yeah, but shoes are good for only one season."

"And if global warming keeps getting worse, then that's all the earth will have. One season. As in, hot."

"Okay, I see your point," Veronica told

him. "But how do you make people read an article about recycled paper?"

"Compare it to how many seasons Principal Weatherbee has recycled his suits?" Kevin suggested.

"That's hilarious." Veronica laughed. "Can you believe it? Kim came over to me in the library yesterday and asked if she could come back and do her dress code story."

"What did you tell her?" Kevin wanted to know.

"I said okay, but I'm not sure what I'm going to do with it."

"Change it into what the dress code should be for Riverdale students that are fashion challenged," he suggested with a grin.

"Perfect!" Veronica told him. "I've got to write all this stuff down."

Kevin stopped smiling when he saw Veronica actually pull out a pen and flip through her notebook. "Um, Ronnie? I hope you didn't take my suggestion seriously. I mean, I thought we were just joking around."

"Well, I wasn't. *The Blue and Gold* is boring

and still in the Stone Age. There really needs to be something drastic to get people reading it, and I think a bit of gossip is just the right answer."

"Making a school paper into a tabloid is a horrible idea. I mean, sure, a horoscope and maybe even some jokes might be fun, but tabloid journalism isn't healthy for anyone."

"Sorry, Kevin," Veronica told him. "I'm editor in chief, so what I say goes. Plus, I've given it a lot of thought, and I really think I'm right about this."

"Trust me, Ronnie, you're not. Just go with the articles the writers submit. If you add the horoscope and then maybe a friendly fashion article, that'll be enough of a shake-up for Riverdale High."

Veronica could see that Kevin was sincere, and she really did appreciate his opinions, even if she didn't agree with them. So she simply said, "Okay, Kevin, I'll think about it."

# Chapter 13

Things were humming along with the fashion show. A lot of girls weren't initially thrilled when Betty announced her going green theme, but they all still wanted to be part of the show, so they quickly got over it. Betty pursued running the show with the same hard work and dedication that she did with everything.

After the first two weeks of heading up the committee, she had already picked the models, ordered the invitations, booked the stage and sound system, hired a stylist, ordered the banner, and bought the decorations. Things were going great, even if Veronica was still giving her the silent treatment. Betty didn't care. She was giving the silent treatment right back at her.

It would be weird not having Veronica even be a model in the show, but Betty was fed up with her best friend's condescending attitude. She couldn't wait for all the famous designers to start having environmentally friendly fashion shows. Then Veronica would have to eat her words.

"Betty, check this out," Archie said, sauntering over to her in the hallway. Bearing down, he flexed his chest muscles. "I've been working out five days a week. I'm going to be superbuff for the fashion show."

"That's great," Betty told him. She wasn't really sure that male runway models were supermuscular, but Archie had a long way to go before his neck became thicker than his head, and she didn't want to discourage him.

"That's nothing." Reggie swaggered over and showed his bicep. "Check this out. It's like iron. I've been working out six days a week."

"Well, on the days when I don't pump iron, I jog," Archie told him.

"I jog to school every morning," Reggie countered.

"Well, I'm going to start working out every day and jog to school and jog home."

"Guys!" Betty interrupted them. "You both look very fit. Just don't overdo it, okay?"

"Okay," Archie and Reggie both agreed, but she could see them shooting each other dirty looks.

"And remember not to show up all sweaty from working out when we have the fittings," she told them. "These are new clothes that we have to return to the store, so we've got to keep them nice."

Betty hurried home after school that day to change her outfit. She didn't have designer labels spilling out of her closet like Veronica, but she could still clean up and put on her best ensemble before checking in with the five boutiques that had agreed to participate in the show.

"Hi, Mary Rose," Betty said as she entered the shop, the door chime announcing her arrival.

"Hello?" the elegant shop owner said, obviously not quite placing her teenage visitor.

"It's me, Betty Cooper. I'm the head of the Riverdale High fashion show," Betty reminded her.

"Oh, that's right," the older woman said. "I was just thinking about you the other day. How are things coming along with the show? Will Veronica be joining you today?" She looked out the window, scanning for Veronica's red car.

"Um . . . things are going great!" Betty said. "But I'm afraid Veronica's busy and won't be joining us."

"Oh," Mary Rose said, obviously disappointed by the loss of a retail opportunity. Veronica could always be counted on for some impulse purchases.

"So, anyway," Betty pushed forward, "I just came by to tell you that our theme this year is going green."

"Green?" the boutique owner repeated.

"That's right."

Mary Rose scanned her shop. "As in the color? I mean, we have a few green items, but not enough to put together more than one or two outfits."

"No." Betty did her best to suppress a giggle. "I mean green like the environment. You know, keeping our planet green."

"Oh." Mary Rose gave her a concerned look. "Green like the environment. Um . . . that's going to be a tough one."

"What do you mean?" Betty asked, alarmed by the woman's tone.

"I mean this is a fashion boutique, not a . . . a . . ." Mary Rose struggled for a good comparison. "Not a booth at an environmental fair."

"I'm sorry, but I thought you'd like the theme. I mean, everybody cares about the environment, right?"

"Of course I care about the environment," Mary Rose snapped. "That's not the point."

"I'm sorry, but then what is the point?"

"Look around the shop." The boutique owner made an expansive gesture. "Show me what I'm supposed to put on the models."

"Well," Betty started off hesitantly, "how

about something made out of silk? That's kind of green, isn't it? And there's . . . um . . . some cotton fabrics if they haven't been chemically treated or dyed or anything."

Mary Rose let out a large sigh. "Listen, Betty, I'm sorry, but I'm afraid I'm going to have to back out of being part of this year's show. I'd like to help out, but a big part of why I do the show is to bring new customers into my shop. I just don't have the clothes to cover your green theme."

"But wait." Betty felt a growing wave of panic. "Just give me a minute to figure something out. I'm sure we can work some of your fashions into the show."

"Sorry." Mary Rose shook her head. "You're going to have to count me out this year. But come see me next year if you decide to do something a little more retail friendly."

Betty's eyes filled with tears as she hurried from the boutique. It had never occurred to her that any of the shops would have a problem with the going green theme. After all, it was about something important: the environment.

Still, Betty bolstered herself, she had four shops left that were willing to participate, and she would just have to approach them in a more positive manner, pointing out how their businesses could benefit from her fashion show theme.

By the time Betty pulled her car into the driveway of her parents' house that evening, she was a complete wreck. Every single shop had dropped out of the fashion show. She had absolutely no vendors.

Betty would happily change the theme to cheetah prints or love letters or any of Veronica's original suggestions, but she'd already ordered the invitations and decorations. She could maybe work with the tablecloths and flower arrangements, but there wasn't room in the budget for a reprint of the invitations. She'd gone all out and ordered them embossed on recycled paper. "What am I going to do?" she wailed as she turned off the ignition and slumped in the driver's seat.

Betty desperately wished she wasn't

fighting with Veronica. She would know what to do. She would see a way to make the vendors participate in the show. At the very least, she would be a shoulder to cry on.

A melody started playing in Betty's purse, and, wiping her eyes, she fished out her cell phone. "Hello?" she said, trying not to sound too forlorn and hoping against hope it was her best friend.

"Hi! It's Ginger."

"Oh, hi. I was just thinking I needed to talk to you," Betty told her, doing her best to keep her voice from wavering. "Are you sure that all the big designers are doing environmental themes this year?"

"Positive," Ginger told her.

"Okay," Betty sniffed. "But would you mind telling me *how* they're doing environmental themes?"

There was a long pause at the other end of the line, and then Ginger finally said, "I'm sorry, Betty, but I have absolutely no idea."

# Chapter 14

Veronica could not wait to get to school that Friday. She'd been putting in megahours at the paper and, finally, the fruits of her labor would be delivered in neat stacks outside of every homeroom—it was distribution day for the latest and greatest issue of *The Blue and Gold.*

As Veronica trotted up the front steps of the school, Ginger swept down on her, waving a copy of the paper. "Ronnie, it's hilarious! The whole school is talking about it! You've really done something special here."

"Do you think so?" Veronica was so thrilled she felt fit to burst. "I put in a ton of hours getting it done."

"Oh, you can tell," Ginger assured her. "You can definitely tell."

"Thanks, Ginger." Veronica was on the verge of bubbling over with excitement. "And I superappreciate all your support and enthusiasm."

"Don't mention it."

Veronica really had put 100 percent of her effort behind the paper. All the writers had turned their articles in on time. But as predicted, a lot of their stories were pretty plain for Veronica's tastes, so she decided she had to spice them up. Kevin had refused to help so, staying up half the night, she took on fixing the problem single-handed. She transformed Kim's article on the school dress code into a searing story about how low-rise jeans were going the way of the dodo bird. She made sure to emphasize how only the extremely fashion challenged still thought they were a hot item. Nancy had tried to use actual astronomy with her astrology horoscopes, and the outcome was a little dry. Veronica took it upon herself to give each prediction a little more zing. For example, when Nancy submitted:

"Sagittarius: The alignment of Saturn with the stars in Orion's belt suggests that this is a good week to start a new venture."

Veronica edited it to read:

"Sagittarius: The stars have aligned to tell you that your old relationship has grown stale. This week is a great time to cast off that boring old beau and pursue a brand-new hunk."

Veronica hurried to her locker. She couldn't wait to get to homcroom and hear what everyone had to say about *The Blue and Gold*.

"There you are!" a voice snarled, causing Veronica to spin around. Kim was clutching a copy of *The Blue and Gold*, her eyes blazing. "What do you call this?"

"That's the school paper," Veronica informed her.

"I know, but why does my article say, 'Don't force your friends to call you a fashion disaster behind your back, ditch those low-rise jeans before they waste your reputation'?

I never wrote that! But here it is in black and white with my name credited as the author!"

"I'm sorry, Kim, but your article needed more zip. I had to make an executive decision, so I changed it."

"I can't believe you did this!" Kim shouted at her. "You completely rewrote my story. Now everyone thinks I'm some sort of fashion snob, when it's actually you! I quit *The Blue and Gold*! You've ruined the paper! I demand a retraction stating that I never wrote this nasty article!"

"Take it easy!" Veronica held up her hands as if to ward off the girl's tirade. "I'm sorry you feel this way. I'll tell everyone I wrote it."

"You'd better!" Kim snarled before stalking off down the hall.

"Geez," Veronica grumbled to herself. "Some people have no sense of humor."

"Hey!" someone said, coming up behind Veronica. It sounded more like an angry greeting than a friendly one, so she was reluctant to turn around. Eventually, she had to peek over her shoulder where she saw

Toño Diaz glaring at her. "What's the big idea with that horoscope in the school paper?" he demanded.

"What do you mean?" she asked cautiously.

"My girlfriend's a Sagittarius. Or, I should say, my ex-girlfriend's a Sagittarius. She just dumped me this morning," Toño fumed.

"Well, what does that have to do with me?" Veronica tried to look as innocent as possible. "I don't write the horoscopes. Nancy does."

"Yeah, but I asked her about it, and she said that wasn't what she wrote. Nancy said that she recommended starting a new venture, but it somehow got edited into 'dump your boyfriend.'"

"You can't blame me for that," Veronica insisted. "No one really believes in horoscopes, do they? It's just supposed to be a bit of fun."

"Yeah, some fun. I get dumped."

"I'm sorry, Toño. Why don't you try talking to her? I'm sure she didn't just decide to break up with you because of the school paper."

"You're probably right," Toño reluctantly agreed. "But I'm sure it didn't help any. You guys should be more careful about what you print in the paper. Words can hurt, you know?"

Veronica promised to be more careful and then scurried down the hall to homeroom. People were talking about *The Blue and Gold*. But it wasn't quite the reaction she had been expecting. By the time she staggered into history class, Veronica was exhausted from fending off angry school reporters and apologizing to offended students. It turned out that a lot of people still liked low-rise jeans and were angry at being told their wardrobe was passé. And that was just the tip of the iceberg as far as their complaints.

"How's it going?" Ginger asked as Veronica collapsed into her seat.

"Awful."

Just then a student aid came into the class. Veronica needed to report to the principal's office right away. "What do you think it's about?" Ginger asked as Veronica gathered her books.

Veronica rolled her eyes and muttered. "I don't even want to find out."

# Chapter 15

Veronica felt very nervous as she hurried down to Principal Weatherbee's office. There had been enough anger and outrage about the paper that it wasn't hard to guess why she was being summonsed. The fact that Ms. Grundy, clutching a copy of *The Blue and Gold*, was sitting in a chair across from Mr. Weatherbee was also a bit of a clue. "Ms. Lodge!" the English teacher said as Veronica entered the office. "Explain yourself!"

"I . . ." Veronica fumbled for words.

"This issue of *The Blue and Gold* is a disgrace!" Ms. Grundy went on waving the paper in the air. "This is the worst issue in the paper's history!"

"But . . . ," Veronica tried again.

"I went over the articles the students handed in, and none of them were this . . . this . . . garbage!"

"Ms. Lodge," Mr. Weatherbee interjected before Ms. Grundy could continue her tirade, "the issue you put out is completely inappropriate for a school paper. What do you have to say for yourself?"

"I'm sorry!" Veronica finally managed to blurt out. "I made a mistake! I thought I was making the paper a little more, you know, modern, but I guess I went too far." She took a big sniff, fighting back the tears that were brimming in her eyes. "I really didn't mean for this to happen. I thought I was making the paper more entertaining, but I screwed up. I'm really sorry."

Mr. Weatherbee appeared to soften, and Ms. Grundy sat back down in her chair. "Well, it's not the end of the world," the principal said in a less severe voice.

"But it is very embarrassing," Ms. Grundy said. Turning to Mr. Weatherbee, she added,

"I think Veronica has bitten off more than she can chew, and she should be relieved of her position as editor in chief."

"No!" Veronica protested. She hadn't wanted to be the editor of the paper, but now that she was, she didn't want to be thrown off the post. "Please don't do that! There's only one issue left this year, and I promise I will do everything I can to make it the best issue *The Blue and Gold* has ever had. Please? Just let me have this chance to make it up to you."

"Well . . ." Mr. Weatherbee hesitated, shooting the English teacher a sidelong glance.

"Fine," Ms. Grundy relented. "But I want to approve every single article *after* you've edited them. Not before. And I want article approval. And no more horoscopes. And . . ."

"I think Veronica gets the point, Ms. Grundy," the principal assured her.

"Well then, fine. Veronica, you're still the editor, but I'm holding you accountable," the English teacher said in her best no-nonsense voice.

"I understand," Veronica assured both of them. "I'll do a good job. I promise." Hurrying back to history class, Veronica wondered why she had fought to stay on as editor. A few weeks ago she didn't even want to be part of the paper, but just a few minutes earlier she had been fighting to keep her position. It just didn't make sense, but a huge part of Veronica wanted to prove that she could actually put out a good issue of *The Blue and Gold*.

Veronica got back to history just as the bell rang signaling the end of class, so she turned on her heel and headed for her locker. Students came flooding out of all the classrooms.

"Looks like Betty and Veronica getting what they deserve," Ginger laughed to Brigitte.

"What do you mean?" Brigitte asked.

"Well, you know how Betty and Veronica cheated to win the school elections?"

"Um, no. They didn't cheat," Brigitte told her.

"Oh, yes, they did!" Ginger insisted. "I saw them standing in the hallway with two ballot boxes, and no one else was around. How else do you explain them both winning?"

"But Ronnie ran to head the fashion show, and Betty ran to edit the paper. If they cheated, then don't you think they'd cheat so they'd win the offices they actually wanted?"

"So?" Ginger shrugged. "They stuffed the ballot boxes and then somehow the boxes got switched. I saw them standing right there at the voting booth. They had plenty of opportunity to do it."

"I think you're right about the boxes getting switched, but that was because of Jughead. He was running down the hall with too many boxes and crashed into me. Some of the labels fell off, and I guess he stuck them on the wrong boxes," Brigitte explained.

"Well, then they stuffed the ballot boxes before Jughead got to them."

"No." Brigitte shook her head. "I saw Betty and Veronica right after Jughead knocked me down. They were guarding the ballot boxes for the football uniforms and something else. I can't remember what it was, but it wasn't the boxes for the fashion show or the paper. I know that for a fact. I'm sorry, Ginger, but you're wrong."

"But . . ." Ginger suddenly felt a little wobbly about her convictions. "I know for a fact that they . . . I mean . . . they both won, and I was so sure that . . ."

"Ginger?" Brigitte felt a wave of concern for her friend. "Are you okay?"

"No." The girl shook her head. "I'm not okay. I messed up royally. I've made a huge mistake."

"Well, it can't be that bad. I'm sure it's nothing that can't be fixed."

"Yeah, maybe." Ginger gulped. "But I've really got to talk to Betty and Veronica."

# Chapter 16

"What's she doing here?" Veronica growled as she caught sight of Betty sitting next to Ginger in the teahouse.

"What's she doing here?" Betty said at the same time, springing out of her chair.

It was Saturday afternoon, and Ginger had done a little finagling to get both girls to Leif's Teahouse at the same time. "You guys, listen. Please? It's really important that I talk to both of you, and that's why I asked you here."

Betty slumped back down into her chair. Veronica thought about storming out, but her curiosity got the best of her. "So," she said, giving Betty the stink eye, "what's so important that you have to speak to both of us?"

"Well . . ." Ginger wasn't even sure how to start. "Um . . . Betty, you know how I kind of told you that all the big designers were going to do green fashion shows this year."

"Yeah," Betty replied. "That's why I chose going green as our theme."

"I'm sorry, but that wasn't at all true. I mean, a lot of designers care about the environment, but they show it more through charitable donations rather than actually having environmentally friendly fashion shows."

"What?" Betty couldn't believe her ears. "The fashion show is a complete mess because of the environmental theme! All of the vendors pulled out! I don't even know what I'm going to do!"

"None of the boutiques I set up for you are doing the show?" Veronica couldn't restrain herself from asking.

Betty shook her head sadly. "No one knew how to handle my theme."

"I knew that theme was a bad idea."

"Veronica," Ginger interrupted. "It's not

Betty's fault. I practically tricked her into making green the theme."

"Practically?" Betty was incredulous.

"Okay," Ginger confessed. "I tricked her into the environmental theme."

Betty was on the verge of tears. "That's so mean! Why would you do that?"

"I'm sorry! I got it into my head that you guys cheated, and that was the only reason I wasn't running the fashion show and editing the paper."

"We didn't cheat!" Betty said, wiping at her eyes.

"I know. I know. I figured that out. I was a complete and total jerk, and I'm really, really sorry, you guys."

Veronica furrowed her brow. "Well, what did you do to me?"

"Um . . . I kind of planted the idea in your head of doing the paper in a tabloid style," Ginger confessed with a guilty shrug.

"No, you didn't." Veronica shook her head. "I'm the one that . . . Oh, wait a minute . . ." She remembered the note in history class.

"Sorry." Ginger grimaced.

"Seriously, Ronnie, making a student newspaper more like a tabloid is a horrible idea," Betty assured her.

"Well, it's not as bad as an environmental fashion show," Veronica fired back.

"At least I didn't single-handedly make half *The Blue and Gold* writers quit," Betty countered.

"At least I didn't lose every single vendor!"

"Guys, stop it!" Ginger practically had to shout. "You shouldn't be fighting with each other at all. If you're going to be mad at someone you should be mad at me."

"But . . . ," Veronica tried.

"You two are best friends, and here you are, turning on each other because I tricked you. That's just idiotic!"

Betty and Veronica slouched in their chairs, both chewing over what Ginger had just told them. Finally, Veronica glanced in Betty's direction. "I can understand why you went with the green theme. I mean, I know you're really into the environment, and I think that's great. I should have been a little more supportive about it and helped you pitch it to the vendors."

"Thanks." Betty gave her a wan smile. "And I'm sorry things got so crazy with the paper. Instead of getting upset with you, I should have worked with you to integrate some of your ideas. I guess I was just feeling defensive because I thought you were being really critical about something that's really important to me."

Tossing her long black hair over her shoulder, Veronica sighed. "That's okay. I should have listened to you instead of being so in love with my own ideas."

Ginger smiled. "Okay. Good. Are you friends again?"

"Yeah." Veronica shrugged.

"Sure," Betty agreed.

"Great. Now, let's put our heads together and figure out how to save the fashion show and put out an awesome paper for *The Blue and Gold*'s final issue this year."

"Um, Ginger?" Betty gave her a hesitant look. "I appreciate you confessing and all, but why should we trust you now? I mean, you're the one that kind of screwed things up in the first place."

"Yeah," Veronica agreed.

"I know, but I'm going to do my best to make things right, I swear." She held up her hand as if she'd been called to testify in court. "I'm sorry, you guys. I really am. Can you forgive me?"

Betty and Veronica had one of those silent conversations that can only take place between sisters, best friends, and couples that have been married for fifty years. Finally Veronica said, "All right. We forgive you." Then she added with exaggerated menace and a diabolical voice, "But we're keeping an eye on you." All three girls broke out in giggles.

"Thanks, guys." Ginger was wearing a big grin. "I promise I'm never going to be such a giant jerk ever again."

"That's great, because jerk doesn't look good on you," Betty told her. "So what are we going to do about the fashion show?"

"Change the theme?" Veronica suggested.

"It's too late. I've already got the banner, the decorations, and the invitations."

"Okay, that's a problem, but all we really need to do is come up with a way for boutiques to participate in a show with the green theme."

"I know that, Ronnie, but it's easier said than done," Betty grumbled.

They all sat there pondering the problem for several minutes. Finally, Veronica looked up. "Hey, I know. Have either of you ever heard of these kinds of stores called resale shops? Apparently, people consign their nice clothes that they don't want anymore to the shop and then other people buy them."

Veronica looked so sincere that Betty and Ginger had to suppress their amusement that she thought of resale shops as being such a mystery. "Sure, Ronnie. I know what a resale shop is," Betty told her. "As a matter of fact, I got that blouse I wore yesterday from a resale shop."

Totally amazed, Veronica said, "You're kidding? That was so cute! I wondered where you got it, but we weren't talking, so I didn't ask." Then she went on, "Anyway, reselling something is kind of like recycling, isn't it? So maybe these resale shops might want to be vendors at the show. Their clothes are green because they're not adding to garbage dumps or hurting the environment. What do you think?" Betty and Ginger both turned to stare at her. "What?" she asked.

"Ronnie!" Betty exclaimed. "That's a fantastic idea!"

"It is?" Veronica blushed.

"Genius!" Ginger assured her.

XOXO

The door chimed as the three girls entered Guinevere's Second Chances, an expansive resale shop that Veronica had never even realized existed. Betty and Ginger sailed on inside, but Veronica edged in slowly, looking around the massive shop like she were exploring an uncharted region of the Amazon. After taking in her surroundings for several moments, she straightened up and said, "It's really nice in here."

"Of course it is." Betty gave her a look of

mild concern. "What were you expecting?"

"I'm not sure." Veronica touched the fabric of a black velvet cape that was hanging as part of a wall display. "I guess I thought it would smell a lot more musty or something. This is just like a regular shop."

"Only cheaper," a saleslady said, coming out from behind the counter to greet them. "Hello, girls. Are you just browsing or looking for something special?"

"Are you Guinevere?" Betty asked.

"Yes, that's me. I'm the proprietress. How can I help you?"

"Well." Betty bit her lip. "We're part of the Riverdale High School Charity Fashion Show, and we're looking for boutiques that might want to participate this year."

"Oh." The woman smiled hesitantly. "As you know, this is a resale shop. Are you sure I have the kind of styles you're looking for?"

"Definitely," Betty assured her. "Our theme this year is going green, so we're looking for vendors who are environmentally friendly."

"There would be a lot of free publicity,"

Ginger added. "And maybe some kind of tax write-off or something. I'm not sure, but it is for the children's hospital."

"And free advertising in *The Blue and Gold*," Veronica offered.

"What's that?" Guinevere asked.

"It's our high school's paper, but it has a lot of readers."

"So." Betty cast an eager eye around the shop. "You've got a lot of great stuff here. Do you think you'd be interested?"

Guinevere pursed her lips and gave it some thought. "You know what? I think I would."

XOXO

There were three resale shops in Riverdale, and all three eagerly signed up to have clothing in the fashion show. As they walked out of the third shop into the early evening air, Betty danced around the parking lot. She couldn't believe how quickly her luck had turned. Veronica was her best friend again, and she actually had people enthusiastic about having their clothing in her environmentally friendly fashion show. It was just plain incredible! "I really can't believe it," she exclaimed to her friends. "This is such a relief! I was totally freaking out about the fashion show, and now I'm all excited about it again."

"Wish I could say the same about the paper," Veronica said, shifting her shopping bags from one hand to the other. She had managed to buy something in every shop. "You have never seen Ms. Grundy as angry as she was with me about the last issue. Normally, I think she's pretty nice, but let me tell you, she can get really intense."

"Well, she's been helping with the school paper since she started teaching at Riverdale High," Betty informed her.

"Back when we were just forming our nation," Ginger added. "They had only hand-cranked printing presses." Betty and Veronica both stopped and gave her a double take. Ginger cracked into a smile. "Just kidding."

"But seriously," Veronica went on. "What am I going to do about the paper? Most of the writers quit over the last issue."

"Well, I could talk to some of the writers,"

Betty offered. "I'll explain how you're repenting your tabloid ways, and you really need some great articles."

"Do you think that would work?"

Betty shrugged. "It might work. A lot of people really love working on the paper, so they probably wish they didn't quit. I guess it wouldn't hurt to try."

"That would be so great!" Veronica gave her best friend a one-armed hug as they walked along. "I superappreciate it."

"Of course." Betty smiled. "And I'm going to contribute an article, too, you know. Something about . . . Well, I haven't thought of a good idea yet, but I will."

"Me too," Ginger chimed in. "I know exactly what I want to write about for the next issue of *The Blue and Gold*."

"What?" Betty and Veronica both asked, a bit of anxiety hanging in their voices.

Ginger broke into a crooked grin. "The fashion show, of course."

# Chapter 17

As Veronica climbed the stairs to Riverdale High, eager to get her hands on the latest copy of *The Blue and Gold*, she couldn't help but flash back to the last morning an issue of the paper was going to hit the homerooms. She had been so excited, so overconfident, and then so very miserable. It would be interesting to see how the other kids reacted to the final issue of the paper for the school year. Betty had worked miracles, getting almost every writer to return to the paper. They all took such care and such pride in their work. Veronica felt ashamed that, the first time around, she had so callously rewritten everything without any consideration for their feelings. At least she'd tried to make it up to them. This time she went over every submitted article with a fine-tooth comb, but looking for only small tweaks to make the articles read better or for obvious grammatical errors. Veronica had to admit she didn't find many. *The Blue and Gold* writers obviously took the paper seriously.

And she felt better about having excised the tabloid out of the paper. Gossip, even in jest, wasn't really good for anyone. Veronica wondered how movie stars must feel having their weight gains and breakups and fashion blunders plastered across the fronts of magazines. It probably hurt, even if the people were famous. The thought almost made her decide to end her subscription to *You Weekly*. Almost.

The first person Veronica saw from the paper's staff was Nancy, getting some books out of her locker. Veronica wasn't sure if she should say hi or just pretend she hadn't noticed the other girl. Before she could make up her mind, Nancy noticed her instead. "Hey," she called. "I just got a peek at the latest issue." Veronica held her breath, waiting for the other shoe to drop. Nancy had been reluctant to return to the paper, but Betty had persuaded her. "It looks really good!" Nancy exclaimed. "Ginger's article is awesome, and I'm so glad you were able to talk Ms. Grundy into letting me try again with the horoscopes. They're actually really fun to write."

Veronica let out a sigh of relief. "That's great."

"And thanks for encouraging me to put a little more zing in my predictions. I really think I made them more fun to read this time."

A big smile spread across Veronica's face. "No problem. And thanks for giving me a second chance as editor. I really appreciate it."

Nancy smiled back. "No prob."

"Oh." Veronica lowered her voice, just in case anyone had decided to eavesdrop. "And thanks for customizing that one special thing we talked about."

"My pleasure," Nancy whispered. "I like playing cupid. And please let me know if it works."

Students were reading *The Blue and Gold*. Lots of students. In fact, several of them came up to Veronica between classes and said they enjoyed the issue. Ms. Grundy even pulled Veronica aside after English class to tell her she was proud of her. "This may be one of my favorite issues of *The Blue and Gold* in the last decade."

"Thanks, Ms. Grundy." Veronica glowed. "I'm just happy I could do the paper justice."

As Veronica was switching out her books at her locker after English class, Toño Diaz came bounding up to her and wrapped her in a giant bear hug. "Oof! Hi, Toño," she wheezed.

"Veronica, you're a genius!" he crowed.

"I am?" She had to bend slightly at the waist to regain her breath.

Toño pulled a copy of the school paper out of his back pocket. It was folded open to the horoscopes. Finding the Sagittarius entry, he read, "Now is the time to look back at past loves. That old suitor that you hastily rejected is well worth a second chance."

Veronica couldn't help but grin. "Yeah, I asked Nancy to put that in there special. I figured it was the least I could do."

"Yeah, Nancy told me. And I wanted to tell you, it worked. My ex-girlfriend is now my girlfriend again."

"That's terrific." Veronica patted him on the shoulder. "But, Toño, you're a great guy. Are you sure you want to keep dating a girl that's so influenced by astrology?"

"Uhhh . . ." Toño considered the problem. "You've got a point. But she is awfully cute. And at least now if we break up, I'll know it's for legitimate reasons and not to push copies of *The Blue and Gold*."

As Toño went in search of his off-again on-again girlfriend, Betty came rushing down the hall. "Ronnie! You're not going to believe it!" Veronica didn't even have time to ask what was going on before her friend continued. "All of the tickets to the fashion show have sold out! In fact, we even sold out the standing-room-only tickets. The show is filled to capacity! If we sell any more tickets, we won't be able to fit everyone in the gym!"

"Are you kidding?" Veronica couldn't believe her ears. "Sold out? That's incredible! I mean, the show has always sold pretty well, but never sold out. And with standing room only? That's amazing! I can't believe it!"

"I know!" Betty's face was pink with excitement. "I can't even begin to figure out how this happened. I mean, there are people actually driving in to see the show."

"Driving in? Driving in from where?"

"Driving in from everywhere!"

The two friends joined hands and jumped around in a circle they were so excited. "We've got to find Ginger!" Veronica exclaimed. "Maybe she knows why this is all happening." Just then, Ginger rounded the corner.

"Ginger!" both girls called out to her.

"You'll never guess what!" Betty added.

"What?" Ginger's eyes were round with wonder.

After Betty had explained about the ticket sales for the fashion show, there was more squealing and jumping. "I had a feeling this would happen," Ginger said happily. "I got a ton of comments on my blog."

"On your blog?" Veronica stopped bouncing and gave her a questioning look.

"Yeah, I've been writing about the fashion show on my Teen Sparkle blog every day for the past two weeks."

"Oh!" Veronica nodded her head. "I bet that's why so many people from out of town are coming to the show."

"That was really cool of you," Betty said, giving her a one-armed squeeze.

"Well, it was the least I could do after causing you guys so much trouble." Ginger cast her eyes down, looking slightly shamefaced.

"Let's just forget about that now," Betty insisted. "The paper turned out great, and now I just want to focus on making the fashion show superfantabulous!"

Just then, Archie came limping down the hall. Veronica caught sight of him first. Hurrying over to help him, she called, "Archiekins! What happened? Are you hurt?"

"No," Archie grimaced. "Just sore from working out."

"Well, you shouldn't work out to the point that you're in pain."

"I don't normally," Archie admitted, "but I want to be pumped up for the show. Reggie's really been looking buff lately, and I don't want him to show me up. Could you girls point me toward the gym? I want to sneak in a workout during independent study."

"Archie." Betty gave him a concerned look. "You don't need to work out anymore. The best thing you can do is relax and get a good night's sleep. That way you'll look fresh for the show."

Shaking his head, Archie started limping toward the gym. "Just one more workout should do it. Then I'll go to bed early. I promise."

The three girls pondered his back as Archie dragged himself toward yet another workout. "Boys are so weird," Ginger mused.

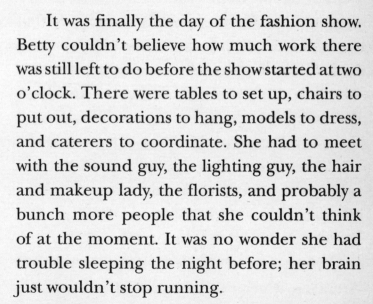

# Chapter 18

It was finally the day of the fashion show. Betty couldn't believe how much work there was still left to do before the show started at two o'clock. There were tables to set up, chairs to put out, decorations to hang, models to dress, and caterers to coordinate. She had to meet with the sound guy, the lighting guy, the hair and makeup lady, the florists, and probably a bunch more people that she couldn't think of at the moment. It was no wonder she had trouble sleeping the night before; her brain just wouldn't stop running.

As Betty drove toward the school, she couldn't get over her relief that she and Veronica were friends again. Not only was it great to get her best friend back, but Veronica was a dynamo of fashion coordination. She really knew who needed to do what and how to keep things moving.

By five minutes to one, the Riverdale High School gym was crawling with people setting things up, taping crepe paper to rafters, and coating hair with hair spray. Almost everything was in place, and they were ahead of schedule. There was only one hitch that Betty couldn't quite figure out. "Where are Archie and Reggie?" she wondered aloud as Veronica sat down next to her to take a well-earned break. "They were so excited about the show. I thought they'd be early, not late."

"I don't know." Veronica pulled out her cell phone and tried Archie's number. "I've called like five times."

"There's Reggie." Betty pointed. "Where have you been?" she called. "Where's Archie?"

"I have no idea," Reggie wheezed as he dragged himself over to where the girls were sitting. He was going to say something else but was prevented by a coughing fit.

"You sound really bad, Reggie. Are you sick?" Veronica got to her feet and tried to peer at his face. "You're all blotchy. Do you have a fever?"

"No, I'm fine," Reggie insisted, blowing his nose. "I'll be fine."

"How can you say you're fine when you've turned into a human snot factory?"

"It's not that bad," Reggie managed to get out before he went into another bout of coughing.

Betty put her hand to Reggie's cheek. "You're burning up," she told him. "You need to go home and get in bed."

"I'm fine," Reggie told her between coughs. "Seriously, I can do the show."

Betty shook her head. "No, you can't. It's too risky with a fever. And besides, I don't want you infecting everyone else in the show. Go home, Reggie. Now."

Reggie didn't try to argue with her. He just mumbled, "Sorry, Betty." As he went out, Archie stumbled in, looking just as pale and splotchy as his friend.

"Archie, not you, too!" Veronica cried.

"What?" Archie straightened his spine and tried to act like he wasn't feeling miserable.

"You're sick," Veronica said. "I can tell just by looking at you."

"Not at all," he insisted. "I feel great. I'm just a little tired from working out so much." His statement was followed by half a dozen sneezes, so it didn't carry much weight.

"Go home," Betty told him. "It looks like you and Reggie exercised your way right out of the fashion show."

"I can still do it," Archie whined. "I took some cold medicine."

"Forget it, Archie. Go home, eat some soup, and go to bed."

After Archie shuffled off, the two girls exchanged looks. "What are we going to do? I was counting on Archie and Reggie. Why did they have to work out so much?" Betty wailed.

"Did you tell them they had to get in shape for the fashion show?"

"No, I never encouraged them." Betty sighed. "They just started exercising."

"Boys are a mystery," Veronica told her. Then, giving her a bolstering slap on the back, she said, "Come on. I think we can figure something out."

Jughead was steadying a ladder while Kevin tried to adjust the welcome banner that was hanging a bit cockeyed over the school's entrance. "A bit higher on the left," Jughead called up to him.

"That looks awesome," Betty said. "You guys are doing a great job."

Kevin smiled down at her. "Let us know if you need anything else."

"Well, now that you mention it." Betty returned his smile. "There is one thing . . ."

XOXO

"Absolutely not!" Jughead said as soon as he'd heard Betty and Veronica's plan to turn him into a male model. "I'm here to hold the ladder, eat the leftover snacks, and maybe take a nap behind the bleachers. That's it!"

"Oh, come on, Jughead. Please?" Betty begged.

"No way! I'm not some fashion plate

that you girls can parade around at your convenience," he insisted.

"Well, what about you, Kevin?" Veronica asked. "Will you help us out?"

"Sure, I guess." Kevin shrugged. "If you're really stuck."

Narrowing her eyes and glancing at Jughead, Veronica said in a casual voice, "That's so sweet of you, Kevin. Because it's so last minute and everything, why don't we take you out to Pop's Chocklit Shoppe for a burger after the show?"

Kevin caught on immediately. He did his best not to laugh or look in Jughead's direction. "A burger? That sounds great."

Betty joined in the luring. "I'll even throw in fries and a shake."

It was only a few seconds before Jughead reached his breaking point. "That's not fair!" he protested. "No one told me there was going to be burgers!"

"Oh, I didn't think about it. Does it matter?" Veronica gave him an innocent look.

"Burgers always matter," he assured her.

"If you're willing to feed me after the show, then you can dress me up in any silly outfit you want."

Betty hurried the guys backstage to get ready. There were only forty minutes before the guests would start to arrive.

XOXO

"The show is going great," Veronica whispered as she and Betty, both standing backstage, peeked through the curtain.

Midge, Ethel, and Brigitte had all just exited from the runway, looking fabulous. "Nice job, girls," Betty whispered to them.

Kevin was on the runway, showing off a pair of gabardine slacks and a slim-fit, button-down navy shirt. The blue in the top brought out the blue in his eyes and made them sparkle. He paused at the end of the stage and then did a pivot turn. As he headed back up the catwalk, Jughead passed him, looking stylish in a black turtleneck and dark blue jeans. He was adamant that he was able to wear his crown beanie, which kind of threw off the whole James Bond–style he was supposed to be projecting, but he still looked good. "The clothes look so fantastic." Veronica nodded her approval. "I never would have guessed they were from a resale shop."

"I can't believe we pulled off a green fashion show. It's incredible!" Betty marveled.

"I can't believe I put out an issue of *The Blue and Gold* that made Ms. Grundy happy," Veronica countered. "Thank you so much for helping me win back the writers."

"No problem," Betty told her.

"You know," Veronica went on. "At first I didn't want to do the paper at all, but once I started working on it, I really did enjoy it. I mean, it was megachallenging and everything, but in a good way. Do you know what I mean?"

"Totally," Betty assured her. "I feel the same way about the fashion show. I guess it's good to get out of your comfort zone every once in a while and try new things."

"Yeah, but it really helps to have your best friend there in case you totally screw up."

Betty enthusiastically nodded her head. "No kidding."

# Epilogue

Finals were barreling down on the students of Riverdale High, and the excitement of a fast-approaching summer vacation was, too. "I can't believe how much studying I have to do in the next two weeks," Betty groaned as she paged through a notebook.

"Well, there's no one saying we can't do our studying poolside," Veronica told her. "We might as well work on our tans while we work on our finals."

"Girls! Guess what?!" Ginger came charging down the hall toward them, waving a copy of *Sparkle Magazine*.

"What?" Betty and Veronica asked.

"Wait, let me show you." Ginger skidded

to a stop and then began thumbing through the issue. She found the page she was looking for and said, "Here, read this."

Betty squinted at the magazine and read the headline of a small article in the What's Happening section: "Riverdale Geeks and Chics Shine in Green Fashion Show." Then she looked up at Ginger. "You wrote an article about the fashion show for *Sparkle Magazine*?!"

"It was a last-minute addition. I didn't want to tell you about it until I was sure it would get in."

"But why? How?" Veronica asked.

Ginger broke into a huge grin. "I told you I got a lot of comments on my blog, so they let me put it in." Then she turned to Betty. "You know, you might actually have started a trend. I think some designers will start going green."

"I'm a trendsetter." Betty laughed.

"I know!" Veronica gave her best friend a hug. "I'm going to have to start taking my fashion advice from you from now on!"